THE MAN OF BRONZE

Doc Savage practices one of the most unusual professions ever pursued by a man. Doc Savage is a modern Galahad. He goes around mixing in other people's troubles, aiding the oppressed, righting wrongs, meting out his peculiar brand of justice to evil-doers. He never takes pay from those whom he aids. But he has managed to amass wealth until no one knows how much he controls.

THE SOUTH POLE TERROR

THE
SOUTH POLE
TERROR

A DOC SAVAGE ADVENTURE

BY
KENNETH ROBESON

SOUTH POLE TERROR

*A Bantam Book / published by arrangement with
The Condé Nast Publications Inc.*

PRINTING HISTORY

Originally published in DOC SAVAGE *Magazine 1936*
Bantam edition published February 1974

Published simultaneously in the United States and Canada

*Bantam Books are published by Bantam Books, Inc. Its trade-
mark, consisting of the words "Bantam Books" and the por-
trayal of a bantam, is registered in the United States Patent
Office and in other countries. Marca Registrada. Bantam
Books, Inc., 666 Fifth Avenue, New York, New York 10019.*

PRINTED IN THE UNITED STATES OF AMERICA

Contents

Chapter I

DEATH ON THE SLOOP

DOC SAVAGE happened to be only one of a few million persons who heard about the mystery of the silver sloop almost at once. When it first came to Doc Savage's notice, the mystery probably baffled the bronze man as much as it did any one.

A coast guard patrol boat picked up the silver sloop on Long Island Sound. It was night. The coast guard hailed the sloop because the craft was carrying no lights. Hailed, and got no answer. The silver sloop was a silent ghost with slatting canvas. So the coast guard boarded it.

Next morning, it was in all of the newspapers. They put out extra editions in London. Paris and Berlin sheets had it on the front pages. In remote Japan, they brushed it in queer-looking characters on the public news boards.

Doc Savage, of course, read the papers. Long ago, Doc Savage had found it advisable to keep a close check on the news events of the world. This precaution had on several occasions saved Doc Savage's life. The fact that it had was due to the highly unusual profession which Doc Savage practiced.

The silver sloop was approximately fifty feet long, and she was a fine hooker with teakwood decks, jib-headed sails with roller reefing gear and the rest of the newfangled gadgets. She was all mahogany and shiny metals inside. She was a honey. She made sailors grin from ear to ear and murmur in admiration when they boarded her.

The coast guardsmen were sailors. But when they went aboard the silver sloop, they turned white with horror; some leaned over the rail and were sick.

It was an incredible thing which they found aboard the

silver sloop. The thing was so horrible that no newspaper photographers were allowed aboard after the silver sloop was towed into New London harbor.

The American public, whether they know it or not, are often preserved from sights that might turn their stomachs or keep them awake nights.

What the coast guard found aboard the silver sloop would probably have kept a good many people from sleeping nights. It did the coast guardsmen.

A dead man was found in the steering cockpit of the silver sloop. He was a well-known banker and philanthropist—a man who had been known for his kindliness, his gentle manners.

This kindly soul's dead hand was gripping the hair of a woman whose throat he had cut from ear to ear, and who, later investigation brought out, had been blackmailing the philanthropist for years over an episode of his youth.

The coast guardsmen searched farther and found more horror.

THERE had been fifteen people aboard the silver sloop, a later inquiry disclosed. Fourteen of the fifteen were found, and all fourteen were dead. There was only the one murder, however.

Close examination revealed no wound on any of the bodies, except the cut throat of the woman who had been murdered by the man she had tormented.

At first, the coast guardsmen thought it was poison gas or something, but they found nothing to bear out that assumption. All fifteen persons aboard the silver sloop when she had sailed were identified and they were all either nice or famous people, wealthy for the most part. Even the crew had been decent fellows. Moreover, while one person had died by visible means, there was a great deal of doubt about what had killed the others.

Physicians were naturally called aboard to make an examination. Detectives came, also. They learned a few things.

All the victims had a case of fierce sunburn. But the previous day had been a scorcher for late fall, and the sunburns escaped attention.

The ship's clock had been knocked off the hook by

some one at three o'clock, for it had stopped at that point. Presumably this was three o'clock the previous afternoon.

The tarlike seam compound had been squeezed out of some of the deck's seams. A journalist wrote a wild story about it looking as if a giant hand had seized the craft.

The other point was the most interesting.

One person was missing.

That there was a missing individual was realized immediately that it became known that fifteen persons had sailed aboard the silver sloop for a day's outing on the Sound. A check was made of the names of those sailing.

Velma Crale was the missing name.

Velma Crale's name went into the newspaper headlines with a bang. Velma Crale was famous already; she was the outstanding he-woman of the day. She had flown the Atlantic, the Pacific. She had brought legendary white Indians out of the Amazon wilds. She had received the keys to New York City and had dined with the president.

Velma Crale's latest exploit had been an exploration by air of the South Polar regions. This project had not been so hot, apparently. There had not been the usual publicity upon Velma Crale's return, two weeks previously. Velma Crale had simply announced that she had discovered nothing of value.

This was unusual. Velma Crale was known as a publicity grabber, a lens louse, a show-off who made a big whoop and holler, even if she had not accomplished much. She maintained she could. do anything better than any mere man, and she was not backward about telling the world.

That Velma Crale should come back from the South Polar regions and say she hadn't done anything worth while had simply floored the newspaper boys who knew her. They had once dubbed her "Thunderbird" Crale. Now they wondered why.

Velma Crale had even seemed reluctant to let the cameramen shoot her really snappy profile.

And now Velma Crale was missing. Gone. And she had left fourteen dead madmen and madwomen behind!

The world began looking for Velma Crale. She was not accused of anything. In fact, it was thought that some of the maniacs must have thrown her off the silver sloop during the holocaust. This theory gathered more weight as time passed, and no trace was found of Velma Crale.

Then Doc Savage heard from Velma Crale.

DOC SAVAGE was known in many far corners of the world, and his was a name calculated to make certain types of shady gentry have a good shake in their boots when they heard it.

Almost every one who had heard of Doc Savage knew that he practiced one of the most unusual professions ever pursued by a man. Doc Savage was a modern Galahad. He went around mixing in other people's troubles, aiding the oppressed, righting wrongs, meting out his peculiar brand of justice to evildoers.

This had not proved to be a very profitable profession for Doc Savage. He never took pay from those whom he aided. But he had managed to amass wealth until no one knew how much he controlled.

But very few knew that Doc Savage was financially able to buy some nations outright.

Doc Savage was known more for his fabulous mental ability, his uncanny mastery of electricity, chemistry, surgery, and other professions. Doc Savage was recognized as one of the most skilled in, not one of these professions, but a number of them.

Doc Savage's physical development came in for attention, as well.

The eighty-sixth floor of one of New York's most impressive midtown skyscrapers was the site of Doc Savage's headquarters—his library, laboratory and trick reception room. Laboratory and library were both so complete that scientists frequently came from abroad to examine them. The place was replete with scientific contraptions.

The telephone robot was one of the contraptions. It was put on the telephone wire when Doc Savage was not there. You called up, and a mechanical voice told you that the bronze man was not there, and that any message you cared to give would be recorded for Doc Savage's attention when he returned.

This device was merely an adaptation of the dictaphone, phonograph and vacuum tube amplifier, all built as one instrument.

Doc Savage spent the afternoon delivering a lecture to an eminent group of paleontologists, leaving the group amazed at some of his research work on the subject. Then Doc returned to his headquarters and found the following conversation recorded on the telephone robot.

"This is Velma Crale," a rather pleasant voice had said. "Something awful is happening, and your help is needed. Later in the afternoon, you will receive a package. Please examine the contents and use your own discretion about what to do."

At the end of this brief advice, the robot had automatically recorded the following words, taken off a mechanical clock which gave the time vocally: "This message was received at 3:10 this afternoon."

Doc Savage played the message back at a quarter to six.

Doc Savage called the package receiving room of the skyscraper. Sure enough, there was a package, addressed to Doc. He had it sent up.

The package was not quite a foot square, wrapped in brown canvas and tied with a copper wire. It was very heavy.

Doc Savage was a cautious individual. Otherwise, he would have died long ago. He put the package under an X-ray machine, to see if it contained a bomb. He switched the X-ray machine on.

There was a stabbing flash, a terrific concussion, and the entire top of the skyscraper seemed to fly to pieces.

Chapter II

THE "REGIS" MENACE

Doc Savage's headquarters had been the scene of violence on other occasions, so newspaper reporters had learned to keep an eye on the place. Half of Manhattan Island heard the explosion, and a goodly number even saw smoke shoot out of the top of the skyscraper, and saw brick and glass fall to the street. Luckily, no one was injured seriously by the falling débris.

Reporters and photographers rushed to the spot. The police were there first, however, and kept every one else out. The journalists did a bit of squawking, but they were not allowed to enter. The police also refused to divulge any information.

Directly, six men in white carried a stretcher out of the skyscraper lobby. The journalists craned their necks. A howl of excitement went up.

The form of a giant bronze man lay on the stretcher, extremely quiet. The features were remarkably regular, and the bronze texture of the skin was distinctive. The flake gold eyes were wide open, unmoving. One hand was not covered by the white shroud.

This hand was amazing. It was long-fingered and perfectly proportioned, and it had an incredible equipment of tendons. It was a hand of fabulous muscular strength.

Every one recognized the figure on the litter. Every one also saw something else.

The bronze head was severed from the body!

For moments, not a newspaper man said a word. They were stunned. They knew some of the perils which the man of bronze had faced in the past, and he had always miraculously escaped. It hardly seemed possible that he could be dead. But the evidence was there before their eyes, although the police made an effort to keep them from observing.

There was no mad·rush for pictures. There was no shouting. The silence was funeral-like. Heads bowed. The litter bearing the form of Doc Savage was placed in an ambulance which was, significantly, black.

Later, questions were asked. Yes, the explosion had all but demolished the laboratory of Doc Savage's headquarters. The form on the stretcher had been picked up in the wreckage. No, photographers could not take pictures. What would be done with the body? That had not been decided yet.

Who was responsible for the blast? Had Doc Savage been experimenting and had an accident?

The police replied that they had nothing to say as yet.

At this point, a man who was not a journalist appeared and tried to get through the police lines. He said he had to see Doc Savage. He was told Doc Savage was dead.

"Velma Crale!" this man exploded.

WHEN the man gasped the name of Velma Crale, it was the signal for sharp attention from a policeman who overheard it.

"What'd you say?" the cop demanded.

The stranger who had made the exclamation had bony hands and a face that made one think of a Shetland pony. His hair was blond and stood up like the bristles on a scrub brush. His eyes were remarkably blue. His expensive clothing did not fit him any too well.

"Eh?" he muttered evasively to the policeman. "What do you mean?"

"Didn't you say something about Velma Crale?" asked the officer. "Velma Crale is the one person missing off that silver sloop loaded with dead madmen and madwomen."

The bony, blond man shook his pony-like head violently.

"I said, 'Oh, my—hell!' " he said. He spoke it again, "Oh, my—hell!"

It did sound as if he might have said that instead of "Velma Crale!" The officer was almost satisfied.

"Who are you?" the cop questioned.

"Derek Flammen," replied the other.

The officer frowned, scratched his head, then brightened.

"The South Pole explorer!" he exclaimed.

"The same," agreed Derek Flammen. "I was interested in getting Doc Savage to finance me in an exploration of the South Polar continent. I came to see him for that purpose."

The cop bowed his head.

"I'm sorry," he said.

Derek Flammen groaned, "So Doc Savage is dead!"

"They just took the body away in a hearse," said the policeman.

"This is hideous!" groaned Derek Flammen.

Then Derek Flammen moved away.

The policeman who had talked with Derek Flammen also moved away. He entered the skyscraper, picked up a telephone, and spoke.

"I've got something to report that might be of interest."

"Go ahead," an expressionless voice told him.

The officer repeated exactly what had been said between himself and Derek Flammen.

"The guy might have said, 'Oh, my—hell!' instead of 'Velma Crale!' " he finished.

"Thank you," said the expressionless voice.

DEREK FLAMMEN was collared by a newspaperman before he left the vicinity of the skyscraper. The spotlight of publicity frequently fell upon Derek Flammen's name, because he was a rather well-known figure in the realm of exploration.

Since Doc Savage had been a famous explorer, Derek Flammen was asked to make a statement on the bronze man's death. Derek Flammen thought for a moment, then made his statement.

"The world little knows the true importance of the lifework of the man of bronze," he said, "but it will long remember. It is my prediction that the grindstone of time, which dulls the memory of most celebrities, will but etch more sharply the name of Doc Savage. His character was a diamond which will cut sharply through the ages. Mankind has to-day suffered one of its greatest losses."

"That's a swell statement," said the newshawk.

Derek Flammen worked through the throng in search of a taxicab. It was dark by now. Not until he reached the outskirts of the throng now about the skyscraper did he find a cab.

He was so interested in the job of locating a conveyance that he did not pay too much attention to his trail. He might easily have been shadowed.

Nor did Derek Flammen seem to be in any great hurry to get to his destination, which he gave as a popular uptown hotel. He sat back on the taxicab's cushioned back seat, and his aquiline face was thoughtful. Once, he made a small sound that might have been a chuckle or a snarl, since his face showed neither hate nor delight.

"Damn Velma Crale!" he said quite distinctly. "I wonder why the hell she was ever born?"

Derek Flammen alighted from the taxi in front of his hotel, paid the driver, smiled at the doorman, smiled at the elevator operator, and unlocked the door to his suite with a key which he had been carrying. The suite was dark. He stepped in and turned on the light, somewhat absent-mindedly.

"You may as well hold that pose!" said a crisp, throaty voice.

Derek Flammen did anything but hold the pose. His hand was still on the light button. He doused the lights. Simultaneously, he jumped to one side. He crouched there.

Came a *swish!* A hard blow hit Flammen's right shoulder. He grunted, struck wildly in the darkness, hit nothing, and changed his position.

Almost instantly, he was struck another blow. He swore. He changed his position a third time. The interior of the room was as black as a bats' cave.

Yet the attacker found him again, unerringly. This time, Flammen was all but stunned by a smash to the side of his head.

Flammen snarled. He had suddenly discovered why the other could see him. His hands. There was a glowing substance on one of them. A phosphorescent stuff, obviously. He glanced at the door and saw where he had gotten it from. Off the inner knob!

"You might as well give up!" advised a voice in the darkness. "Otherwise, I shall start shooting."

"What is the meaning of this?" barked Derek Flammen.

The lights came on.

Derek Flammen stared, blinking, at the single other person in the room.

"Velma Crale!" he gulped.

VELMA CRALE had frequently been called the female Amazon of the twentieth century, because of the feats which she had performed. She did not look the part.

She was a small girl who looked as harmless as a

mouse, and who had, just now, about the same coloring. Her arms did not bulge with muscles, despite the manner in which she had been whacking Derek Flammen about. Her features were regular, but not outstanding.

Velma Crale, just now, did not look like a heart smasher over whom two dignified Englishmen had fought a duel, and for whom an Indian nabob had renounced a province and twenty-two wives. This was because Velma Crale had dyed her hair to a nondescript hue, and was wearing no make-up, besides wearing some very plain clothes.

Velma Crale, when she had on her war paint, was really something to look at. What was more effective, she had glamour, personality, and a nice quota of brains.

Velma Crale was, incidentally, noted for her lack of interest in men. Thus far, her heart had been a rock on which luckless admirers had dashed themselves unavailingly.

She waved the big pistol which she held, and with which she had been clubbing Derek Flammen.

"I've shot men before!" she said, meaningly.

This was true. She had, singlehanded, fought off a war party of cannibals on an occasion when her plane was forced down in a New Guinea jungle.

Derek Flammen wet his lips. He kept his eyes on the gun's muzzle. The girl seemed to be considering her next move. They stood thus for some moments.

During those moments, something happened that neither of the two in the room noticed. The window raised a fraction of an inch. This was especially remarkable since the window opened on the side of the hotel which was sheer for twenty stories down and ten upward.

Derek Flammen sighed loudly.

"You are not going to get away with this!" he growled.

Velma Crale sniffed. It was the same kind of a sniff she would gave a toothless dog who made out as if he were going to bite.

"You are as conceited as all men," she said, scathingly. "I'm not afraid of you."

"Not with that gun, you wouldn't be!" Flammen grumbled.

Velma Crale smiled nastily. Then she did a thing which

was indicative of the spirit which had earned her reputation.

She tossed her loaded gun on the bed. Then she walked toward Derek Flammen with her fists up. Flammen looked delighted, lunged for her. His delight vanished. She hit him in the right eye, pulled some hair out of his head, and kicked him in the midriff, all before he could help himself.

The next instant, Derek Flammen was flat on his face, the remarkable young woman seated on his back, holding him with a neat jujitsu hold which dealt awful agony.

"I'm not afraid of anything that wears pants," said Velma Crale.

She searched Derek Flammen, relieved him of a pocketknife and a large, straight-stemmed pipe. She tied his hands and ankles with bedsheets from the bedroom.

Stepping back, she examined the pipe. The inlaid stem interested her. She pointed it at the wall and tried pressing various bits of the inlay.

She got a small *zing!* of a noise. Something hit the wall, and she went over to examine it—a tiny dart.

"Poisoned, I'll bet!" she snapped, and glared at Derek Flammen.

The latter said nothing, but he did not appear to be in a comfortable state of mind.

Velma Crale stamped over and glared at him.

"Where is Thurston H. Wardhouse?" she asked.

"I never heard of such a man!" snapped Derek Flammen.

"Of course not!" Velma Crale laughed, harshly. "But Thurston H. Wardhouse is sailing from Southampton on the liner *Regis* to-night, and when I get my hands on him, plenty is going to happen!"

Derek Flammen kept silent. But he became slightly pale.

"I've been doing plenty of sleuthing around," advised Velma Crale. "I know the whole story. I know just how many millions are at stake."

Derek Flammen swallowed, plainly with some effort, but still did not speak.

"When your crowd tried to run a whizzer on me, you

tackled the wrong person!" snapped the young woman. "I'm going to run you ragged! I'm going to do myself a lot of good in this. And Thurston H. Wardhouse is going to help me. You didn't know that, did you?"

Derek Flammen seemed about to choke.

The window had not opened more than the fraction of an inch which it had risen earlier.

There came a knock on the door.

Velma Crale got her gun from the bed and sidled over to the door.

"What is it?" she asked.

"Telegram," said a masculine voice outside. It sounded like the voice of a youth.

Velma Crale was too foxy to take a chance on what might be an old ruse.

"Shove it under the door," she called.

A yellow telegraph envelope was promptly shoved under the door.

The young woman looked relieved, picked up the telegram, saw the name of Derek Flammen through the transparent window, and tore the envelope open. She plucked out a folded yellow sheet.

Then she gave a loud gasp and fell to the floor.

Chapter III

THE MYSTERIOUS CABLE

A KEY immediately clicked in the door, and the lock tumblers were operated, after which the door opened.

Half a dozen men stepped in silently, and the last one closed the door hastily. The men were quietly dressed, and had the look of outdoor fellows. Their faces were not what could be called "angelic-looking." All of them had a rather pronounced sunburn, or what appeared to be a sunburn.

"Tie her up and gag her," said the leader. "That gas

stuff in the envelope will only knock her out for a minute or two."

The leader stood out from his followers for several reasons. He was bigger, and he looked meaner. He also wore spectacles with unusually thick lenses of a slightly yellowish glass.

A man bent over the girl. He promptly made a gasping sound and all but fell, then managed to stumble to one side.

"Hell, Cheaters!" he gulped. "Some of that stuff is still in the air!"

"Drag her to one side to tie her and gag her," ordered the leader, answering to the cognomen of "Cheaters."

His unusual spectacles made it no mystery why he happened to be called Cheaters, this being a slang term sometimes applied to glasses.

The orders were carried out on the girl, and none too soon; for she began to mumble from behind the gag, and her eyes sparkled irately.

Derek Flammen rolled and wrenched at the sheets with which his wrists and ankles had been tied by the young woman.

"Turn me loose!" he barked.

Cheaters leered at him.

"Take it easy, blondy!" he growled. "You ain't out of the woods yet."

Derek Flammen relaxed, a peculiar expression on his ponylike features.

"I am at a loss to understand what this is all about," he said.

"That's swell," said Cheaters, ominously. "If you understood, you would probably be at a greater loss. You would lose your life."

CHEATERS now went over to Velma Crale.

"I don't think you'll be squawking for the police," he said. "They're looking for you for sending that bomb to Doc Savage. The attendant in the skyscraper's package room remembered that it had your name on the return address. It's all in the extra editions of the newspapers."

He ungagged Velma Crale.

The young woman stared at Derek Flammen.

"I thought you were the leader of the other mob—of this outfit!" she said in a puzzled manner.

"I don't know anything at all about anything!" snapped Flammen.

Cheaters nudged the girl gently with a toe. "You know me?"

"Cheaters Slagg!" she grated. "You're a rogue; and you'll eventually get hung!"

"After you, my dear," grinned Cheaters. Then he scowled. "On second thought, I don't think we'll give them a chance to hang you. Even though they'd probably lynch you for killing Doc Savage, in spite of the fact that you're a woman."

Velma Crale sniffed. "Nuts to you."

She did not sound very enthusiastic.

Cheaters Slagg rocked on his heels. He lifted his thick, colored spectacles and rubbed his eyes as if they ached. This gesture was, in fact, a habit with him.

"So Thurston H. Wardhouse is working with you now?" he growled.

"No," Velma Crale said, promptly.

"We listened outside the door, so don't lie about it!" retorted Cheaters Slagg. "We've been shadowing you for days, my female go-getter, and we have copies of the cables you've sent to Wardhouse. We know Wardhouse is taking the liner *Regis* to-night."

Slagg bent forward suddenly. His ugly face wore an expression far from benevolent.

"We're taking precautions!" he gritted. "Wardhouse will never see New York again!"

The girl nipped her lips and apparently could think of nothing by way of reply.

"Bring them both!" Slagg rapped suddenly.

Velma Crale and Derek Flammen were lifted bodily and borne out of the room. It developed that the mob had a freight elevator waiting, with a frightened—and evidently crooked—hotel flunkey in charge. He took them down, then grasped a twenty-dollar bill greedily when it was passed to him.

"I won't say nothing about this!" he gulped.

Cheaters Slagg, seizing an opportunity a moment later,

calmly inserted a long knife into the hotel flunkey's heart from behind.

"Not in this world, you won't say nothing!" growled Slagg, holding the dying man's mouth so that he could not make a sound.

They got out into an alley without being noticed and distributed themselves in two cars which were waiting there.

"A lot of guys are going to get themselves dead if this keeps up," Cheaters Slagg said, calmly. "But my idea is that it's worth it."

THE men were fairly confident of themselves, and, anyway, too much looking around would have been likely to attract attention as they drove out on the street, so they did not notice a shadowy form near the mouth of the alley.

Had they noticed, they would have been interested, for the lurking individual had a very furtive manner. Moreover, the person kept so thoroughly concealed in the shadows that it was impossible to tell whether it was man or woman.

The skulker remained sheltered for a time after the cars had departed. Caution was apparently the motive for this. The Cheaters's mob might have scouts lurking about to keep an eye on the scene.

But apparently they hadn't, and after a bit the blot of shadow moved, faded with other patches of murk, then vanished entirely from the vicinity.

A short time later and some distance down the gloomy street, glass broke on one of the grills that admitted to a sewer flood drain. It was a peculiar flat bottle, and a shoe ground the fragments to bits so that they all dropped out of sight.

A bit later in the evening, a police patrolman chanced to stop near the drain, and twirling his club, absently looked down. He saw a peculiar glow and studied it for some time, even getting down on his hands and knees to peer through the grating. He never did quite decide what he had seen.

Long before curiosity was consuming the officer, however, the clerk for a cable company discovered on his counter a cablegram, together with the exact amount of tolls required for its transmission. The clerk had not seen who had left the message, and it was not signed.

The cablegram was marked urgent, so no time was lost in getting it on the wires. The missive was transmitted by teletype to a transatlantic radio station on Long Island, and from thence it went by air to England, and arrived, in the course of a very short time, at the hotel room of the addressee.

The addressee was a gentleman bearing the good Anglo-Saxon name of William Harper Littlejohn.

Chapter IV

THE MYSTERY AT SEA

"PRETERNATURAL eventuation is an amaranthine potentiality," said William Harper Littlejohn, upon receiving the cablegram.

Which was by way of proving that the gentleman in question never used a small word when he had time to think of a big one. He might simply have said the unexpected can always happen

William Harper Littlejohn, otherwise known as "Johnny," was best described as a long suit full of bones. He came about as near being a walking skeleton as the human anatomy can achieve. The top of his head was extraordinarily large. His clothing naturally did not fit him. A monocle was attached to his lapel with a ribbon.

The monocle was not there for foppish reasons, however; the bony person needed it frequently to look at strange rocks and ancient hieroglyphics.

William Harper Littlejohn was one of the world's most learned archaeologists and geologists. He was in London translating some old tablets for the English national museum.

He opened the cablegram and read it. Then he upset a chair charging across his hotel suite sitting room.

"Renny!" he howled. "Read this, you big-fisted hunk of bone and gloom!"

Which proved what some people did not believe—the man did know a few small words.

He handed the cable to the occupant of one of the two bedrooms. A long, puritanical, utterly gloomy face was about all of this individual that could be seen, for the reason that he was in bed and covered. He glanced over the missive.

"Holy cow!" he said. His voice was like the growl of a big bear in a deep cave.

He read the cablegram again.

"Holy cow!" he said, much louder this time. Then he arose from the bed, and wearing an expression of a man going to a funeral, walked over to the door, and calmly knocked the stout wooden panel out with a single blow of one fist.

This was not a remarkable feat, considering that each of his fists consisted of an approximate gallon of bone and gristle, properly hardened. The rest of him would weigh in excess of two hundred and fifty pounds, none of it fat, but his fists were so large they almost seemed deformities.

"I knew something nice would happen to me when I went to church Sunday," he said.

He still wore the look of a man going to a funeral. This, contrarily enough, meant he was vastly pleased with what the world was offering at the moment.

They both read the cable once more.

BOARD LINER REGIS SAILING FROM SOUTHAMPTON TO-NIGHT STOP LEARN WHAT YOU CAN ABOUT A MAN NAMED THURSTON H WARDHOUSE

"It is not signed," rumbled "Renny," whose full name was Colonel John Renwick on the roster of the International Society of Master Engineers, of which he was a charter member. His favorite act was to slam his great fists through the solid panel of a heavy door.

"A signature would be a superfluosity," said William Harper Littlejohn.

"Holy cow!" boomed Renny. "So it would, Johnny. So it would. Let's start checking on this liner, *Regis*."

The bony Johnny went to a telephone, and after an expenditure of many words, large and small, hung up with a disgusted expression.

"The liner *Regis* sailed thirty minutes ago," he said.

THE liner *Regis* was one of the newer ocean greyhounds of the smaller, faster type. She made the run between Southampton and New York in fast time.

However, the expediency of modern life has demanded that every measure be taken to hurry the transmission of the mails, so it was customary for a seaplane to fly out to sea a number of hours after the *Regis* sailed and drop the late mail aboard.

On this occasion, however, the mail plane landed on the calm sea off the bows of the *Regis,* and two passengers were taken aboard by a lowered lifeboat.

The grizzled skipper of the *Regis* was not happy about the slight delay which this transfer occasioned. He confronted the two strangers.

"This is irregular!" he snapped. "Why in Hades couldn't you chaps have taken a later boat?"

Bony Johnny and big-fisted Renny, not wishing to anger the skipper, looked properly serious.

"It was very important for us to get aboard," Renny boomed.

"Who are you?" demanded the master of the *Regis*.

They told him.

The skipper's attitude changed instantly.

"I am sorry," he murmured. "Doc Savage has a group of five men who have aided him in his peculiar life's work. You are two of them?"

"That's right," Renny agreed.

"And, of course," added the skipper, "you will want to get to New York for the funeral."

"Eh?" thumped Renny. "For what?"

"For Doc Savage's funeral."

Renny and Johnny stood as if stricken. It was the first they had heard of what had happened in New York. They tried to speak, but words somehow slipped them.

The kindly master of the *Regis,* not realizing he had

broken the news, said, "Perhaps you would like to see the extra edition of our shipboard newspaper which was put out on Doc Savage's death?"

"Y-yes," Renny said, thickly, "we'd like to see it."

They read it in the cabin which was turned over to them. The story had come by radio, and it was complete, if abbreviated as to space. They said very little while they read it. They were silent for a long time afterward.

Then they asked for separate cabins. It was a strange request. But they wanted to be alone with their grief. They looked like a pair of ghosts when they ate breakfast together the next morning. They seemed to be able to think of nothing to say.

"Holy cow!" Renny mumbled finally. "It can't be true!"

Johnny put down his knife and fork, got up and stood looking out of a porthole. He spoke over his shoulder.

"The late radio reports say a photographer managed to get a picture of the—of Doc's—of—— Damn photographers!"

They did not finish eating.

"This Thurston H. Wardhouse must have something to do with the mob that did for Doc," Renny mumbled at last.

"Yes," Johnny agreed. "We'll find him."

THEY did not find him. Not immediately, at least. And when they did, it was under under incredible circumstances.

There was no Thurston H. Wardhouse on the passenger list. Questioning uncovered no one who knew of such an individual. If the man was aboard, he was obviously under an assumed name.

Renny tried a ruse, hiring a page to go through the ship repeatedly, crying that he had a radiogram for Thurston H. Wardhouse. It did not work.

Johnny and Renny were hampered by the well-meant sympathy of the *Regis's* passengers, who had heard of Doc Savage, and seemed to think the bronze man's two aides would be eager to recount some of Doc's past exploits.

Eventually, Johnny and Renny found it necessary to

shut themselves in their cabins. They did not want to talk about Doc Savage. The subject was too painful.

To the world, Doc Savage was a man of mystery—a being about whom incredible legends were told. To Johnny and Renny, who had been associated with the man of bronze for some years, Doc Savage was almost as mysterious a person. They knew him perhaps as well as any mortal. Yet they did not know him.

Doc Savage had been trained scientifically from childhood for the unusual work he had undertaken. It was no ordinary course of training which he had received; the greatest scientists, the most learned men in many professions, had contributed to it, and Doc Savage, product of their combined skill, had been an amazing combination of mental wizardry and—because he had taken two hours of intensive exercise each day since childhood—a physical superman.

The bronze man's feats had never ceased to awe even his five aides, who were closest to him.

Three of these five men were supposed to be in New York. Johnny and Renny sent them radiograms, asking for particulars.

No answers came.

"That looks bad!" Renny groaned.

"Preponderantly malignant," Johnny agreed, gloomily.

"The mob that got Doc may have made away with Monk, Ham and Long Tom," added Renny.

Four days passed, and the liner *Regis* neared New York—and then one of the most fantastic things in marine history happened.

There was a fog. The afternoon was chilly, for the North Atlantic, even near the end of Long Island, is never overly warm. Passengers promenaded the decks wearing topcoats.

Then it grew hotter. The passengers began shedding their wraps. They perspired. Below decks, it became unusually warm, so almost every one stepped outside to enjoy the unexpectedly pleasant temperature.

It was not pleasant for long. The heat increased. The shade under the awnings became popular. Fans were turned on, and the bar did a rushing business in cool drinks.

No one was excited as yet. They just thought the ship had entered a belt of unexpectedly balmy temperatures.

Persons who looked toward the sun began to notice spots before their eyes afterward. It was as if they had faced a flame of a welding torch.

There came a time when every one on deck had sought the shade.

Then a steward suddenly emitted a yell, grabbed a fat man and tried to throw him overboard. Sailors seized the steward, after which several persons had a good laugh, it being known that the fat man, a passenger, had been particularly annoying to this steward throughout the voyage. The steward was taken below, mumbling, and locked in the brig.

The incident was discussed as a temporary mental derangement brought on by the abrupt alteration in temperatures.

Then Thurston H. Wardhouse appeared.

Chapter V

THE QUEER SHIP

RENNY and Johnny were standing on the promenade, beneath an awning. Both were in their shirt sleeves, and mopping perspiration. At least, Renny was. Bony Johnny never came much nearer perspiring than would a skeleton.

"This is a danged funny thing," Renny remarked.

"Egregiously enigmatical," agreed Johnny.

"I'm still wondering about that cablegram," grumbled Renny. "Who the blazes sent it? We naturally presumed Doc had sent the thing, but well—it must have been some one else."

"An imperspicuosity," Johnny complained.

Then Thurston H. Wardhouse made his advent. He was

as handsome a man as a Broadway chorus boy, but his features were distorted with fear. He came charging down the deck.

"Get under cover!" he shrieked. "Get into the hold! You're going to die if you don't!"

It was chance that took him near Renny and Johnny. But the latter two might never have known the man's identity had he not squawled something else.

"They've killed Doc Savage!" Thurston H. Wardhouse squawled. "Now they're trying to kill me!"

Renny and Johnny came to life with a bang. They collared Thurston H. Wardhouse. Renny did the seizing, and his big fists squeezed, and Wardhouse bawled out in agony.

"What was that you just said?" Renny rumbled.

"Get below decks!" screeched the man. "Quick!"

"Who're you?" Renny countered.

"Wardhouse!" the man wailed, beside himself. "You damn fools! Don't you realize what is happening?"

Renny shoved his long, puritanical face closer to the other man's.

"No," he said. "But we'd like to know."

"It's the sun!" gasped Wardhouse. "The solar——"

He stopped. Caution had struck through his fog of fright. He wet his lips, trembled, but did not say more.

"Go on," Renny invited.

"Yes, afford aggrandizement," Johnny echoed.

Wardhouse heaved in an effort to free himself, but did not succeed.

"Help!" he screeched unexpectedly. "These men are going to kill me!"

Several members of the *Regis* personnel had been approaching, unnoticed by Renny and Johnny. These fellows now rushed forward, intent on rescuing Wardhouse, who they believed was being molested. The sailors were husky. It was either fight or let Wardhouse go. Renny and Johnny chose to release him.

"Something queer is happening here!" Renny boomed. "Take us to the skipper!"

It was a reasonable request, and in a few moments, they were confronting the worried master of the liner.

Thurston H. Wardhouse spoke first.

"Give your engines full speed and turn back!" he rapped, excitedly. "It's the only thing that will save our lives!"

The skipper was a man steeped in the humdrum of everyday life. The request to turn back sounded preposterous to him.

"This man has gone mad," he said, calmly. "Lock him up."

The sailors started to drag Thurston H. Wardhouse away.

Forward, near the bows, there was a loud explosion. The shock of it shook the entire liner. Every one stared in the direction of the concussion.

A hole gaped in the bows, well above the waterline.

"It's too late to turn back now," said Thurston H. Wardhouse.

THE few moments immediately following the blast forward were filled with tumult. Orders were shrieked, directing that the extent of the damage be ascertained. A number of sailors dashed forward to comply with the command.

Some of these sailors fell to the deck and did not arise. Back along the decks, passengers were dashing out, and some of these collapsed the instant they were outside.

Thurston H. Wardhouse took advantage of the confusion. He gave a violent lunge, freed himself of restraining hands, and sprang down a companionway that admitted to the innards of the liner.

Caution seized the skipper of the *Regis*.

"Wheel hard over!" he barked. "Put her bows on our back course! Give her full speed ahead!"

He had decided to take Wardhouse's advice.

Renny looked at Johnny.

"Wardhouse!" thumped the big-fisted engineer.

"A perspicacitive suggestion," snapped Johnny, and they ran in pursuit of the fleeing man of mystery.

Wardhouse had secured but a moment's start. When Johnny and Renny were inside, where the yelling on deck was muffled, they could hear the fleeing man's footsteps. Wardhouse seemed intent on penetrating to the deepest recesses of the ship.

Renny and Johnny, who were about as unlike as two men could be in physical build, were none the less about equal in speed. They kept close together, and they overhauled their quarry.

"We'll have him in a minute!" Renny rumbled triumphantly, when they caught sight of Wardhouse at the end of a passage.

Wardhouse must have heard. He stopped, yanked up a trouser leg, and got a slender revolver which had been holstered there. It was one of the modern target weapons, shooting a missile of small caliber but high velocity. The weapon emitted bullets with small, wicked reports.

Renny and Johnny flipped into the nearest door, and found themselves in a storeroom from which there was no other exit.

"I'll be superamalgamated!" said Johnny, using the word which was his favorite expression of mental agitation.

Renny pawed vigorously at his eyes.

"Holy cow!" he boomed. "Johnny, are you having trouble seeing? Spots in front of my eyes and that sort of thing?"

"Yes," said Johnny. "An excruciating phenomenon."

They were silent a moment.

"It's this heat," Renny thumped finally. "Something queer about it. You remember the story we read in the newspaper about that silver sloop found in Long Island Sound, with everybody aboard dead?"

Big-worded Johnny made an explosive noise.

"Ejaculations and vociferations!" he gasped. "Do you think something like that could be happening to us?"

"Your guess is as good as mine."

Renny set himself, obviously for a leap through the door.

"Where you going?" asked Johnny.

"I'm gonna see that the radio operator is letting the world know what is happening to this liner," Renny boomed. "You stick on the trail of this Thurston H. Wardhouse."

With that, Renny dived outside. He was not fired upon, although he distinctly saw Wardhouse watching him at the opposite end of the corridor. It seemed that Wardhouse would only use his gun to prevent his own capture.

RENNY knew the location of the radio shack—aft, on the top deck. He headed for it. From time to time, he passed his hands over his eyes. He could hardly see. The sensation was like nothing so much as being blinded by a great arc light.

He could, however, perceive enough of his surroundings to feel an unpleasant chill. Passengers and crew were dashing about madly. Remembering the newspaper reports that those aboard the silver sloop found in Long Island Sound had been insane before they died, Renny looked for evidences of mania here.

He became convinced that the strange heat was *not* driving every one mad. Many persons were acting wildly, but that was to be expected. Every one knew something incredibly out of the ordinary was occurring, by now, and many had become hysterical.

On the decks, there were numerous bodies. The fantastic heat seemed to have the power of overcoming any one who exposed himself to it.

Renny kept under cover. He felt that perspiration was running from every pore. He reeled against the wall of the salon, near a thermometer, and paused to look at it. The temperature was only a little above a hundred and twenty, much to his surprise.

The heat, then, was not wreaking the havoc. It must be something else.

Coming in sight of the radio shack, Renny made the last few yards through the open in a wild dash. He flopped through the radio shack door, and immediately was glad he had come.

The *Regis* carried two radio men on duty at all hours, and both were slumped on the floor, where they had fallen. They were still breathing.

Renny, like Doc Savage's other aides, was a skilled radio operator. He set the transmitter dials of the C. W. transmitter and began to tap out a series of S O S signals.

He was having even more trouble with his eyes. The pupils seemed to be balls of fire. He shut his lids, but it did not help much. He was feeling weirdly dizzy.

"S O S," he transmitted. "*L-i-n-e-r R-e-g-i-s i-n s-t-r-a-n-g-e h-e-a-t z-o-n-e. E-x-p-l-o-s-i-o-n. T-h-o-s-e a-b-o-a-r-d d-y-i-n-g*——"

Renny ended his sending there, because a man had staggered into the shack. He could hardly stand. He was holding his head with both hands.

It was Thurston H. Wardhouse. He looked at Renny.

"I made a hell of a mistake!" he croaked. "I didn't know you were Doc Savage's men! I thought—thought—it was a trick——"

He fell over senseless and did not move.

Renny held his own head, keeping his elbow over his eyes. His brain seemed afire. He turned slowly and grasped the radio key. To get help was imperative.

"*S O S*," he sent. "*L-i-n-e-r R-e-g-i-s h-i-t b-y w-e-i-r-d*——"

Renny interrupted his sending there again. Not willingly. He wanted to go on, felt confident he could.

But he slid to the floor unconscious.

Chapter VI

THE DEATH TRICK

THE fragmentary message which Colonel John Renwick transmitted from the stricken liner *Regis* was not the first word to reach the world. Radio operators are an amiable clan, and frequently carry on a conversation over the air.

One radio man on the *Regis* had been gossiping with the operator of another liner, and had remarked on the heat. He had given some details of what had happened, even advising of the explosion, before he passed out.

New York newspapers, of course, broke out extra editions immediately. Newsboys were pacing the streets, crying them within not much more than thirty minutes.

One of these vending urchins was hailed by, and sold a paper to, a person he did not even see. The transaction was conducted through the crack of a partially opened door, in a section of the city devoted to rooming houses.

The newsboy did not wonder about it unduly, because he supposed the other fellow did not have his pants on or something.

The man who had bought the paper was clothed properly enough. Just why he had used such secrecy was a mystery, although it was true that his physical appearance was enough to scare any one who met him in a gloomy alley.

The man was a little over five feet in height, approximately that wide, it seemed; his long, gristled arms dangled well below his knees; his face was incredibly homely, and all of him was covered with bristles which resembled rusty shingle nails. He bore more of a likeness to a big ape than to a human.

"Monk!" No other name could fit him!

He was Lieutenant Colonel Andrew Blodgett Mayfair, but he had heard the name so seldom he had forgotten what it sounded like.

Monk's looks were deceiving. Actually, he was in a way of being the most widely known chemist in America. He was a Houdini of the test tubes.

Monk read the headlines, the bulletins below.

"Ham!" he yelled in a squeaky voice that might have belonged to a small boy.

"What is it, Monk, you beautiful little cupid?" queried a sarcastic, oratorical voice from the adjacent room.

"Ar-r-r!" gritted Monk. "Cut out that wisenheimer stuff, you overdressed shyster! Something serious has happened!"

The occupant of the adjacent room appeared. He was a slender man, thin at the waist, with a large mouth and a high forehead. Striking thing about him, however, was his clothing.

His afternoon garb was sartorial perfection. The presser must have spent hours over the crease in his striped trousers and dark coat; his linen was crisp, and his barber a master.

"Ham," formally known as Brigadier General Marley Brooks, looked what he was—a quick thinker and possibly the most astute lawyer Harvard ever turned out. He never went anywhere without a plain black cane. This was, among other things, a sword cane—one whose tip contained a chemical that put its punctured victims to sleep.

The two men were now exchanging the kind of looks which usually come before a fight, after which Monk passed over the newspaper.

"Hm-m-m," said the perfectly attired Ham, after reading it. "This means Renny and Johnny are probably up against what might be called a predicament."

"We better do something about it," Monk muttered.

"But we have orders to stay here, where no one knows our address, until we get orders to the contrary," reminded Ham. "If we show ourselves, the newspaper reporters will run us wild wanting interviews on what we, as Doc Savage's aides, thought of him."

Monk waved his arms.

"Heck with that!" he squeaked. "The *Regis* being in trouble is a heck of a lot more important!"

The argument continued while both donned long coats and hats which helped conceal their faces. It was not interrupted as they entered a vehicle which appeared to be an ordinary taxicab, kept in a garage attached to the house.

They squabbled over who was to drive, and who was to ride in the rear as passenger. They exchanged awful insults throughout the ride.

They stopped the car in a miserable street down near the water front and both got out, bristling as if ready to fight. Instead, they walked through a door, down a murky passageway, and through another door, Ham carrying his sword cane which had been behind the door, holding it as if he would like to stick Monk with it.

"Quiet, please," an expressionless voice said. "And no lights."

MONK and Ham fell silent. There was not a great deal of traffic in this section of the city, hence it was comparatively quiet. In this stillness, they could hear small sounds. Voices! But they were very faint, and strangely piping. It might have been the conversation of tiny gnomes over toward the far end of the room.

The Liliputian conversation ceased after a time.

"All right," said the expressionless voice. "What is it?"

"Something has happened to the liner *Regis,* according to the newspapers," Monk grunted. "Here's a late edition."

It was very dark in the room, but the newspaper was taken from his hand, after which a tiny light appeared. This glow was a beam from a flashlight, and it illuminated nothing but a portion of the headlines. The point of light traveled rapidly over the story.

"What's the idea of not having any light in here?" Monk wanted to know. He kept his voice down.

"There may be cracks between the boards covering the windows," the expressionless voice explained. "The mob in the next house might happen to see a light."

Monk chuckled softly.

"They suspect anything?" he queried.

"If they do, they have concealed it very well."

"Have they brought Derek Flammen back yet?" asked Monk.

"Not yet," said the expressionless voice. "When we finally located this hide-out, by spotting the cars on which had been smeared a compound that later in the night became luminous, there were six men there, holding the girl, Velma Crale.

"We managed to plant a microphone and run the wires to this room. What we overheard indicated these men expected the return of some person who is their chief, and had orders to wait there until this boss appeared."

"And he hasn't come?" Monk grunted.

"Not yet," agreed the rather remarkable voice. "They have been waiting almost five days, now. And they are becoming rather impatient."

Monk sighed loudly. "Nothing overheard yet to show what this is all about?"

"Nothing."

The dapper Ham interposed, "What are we going to do about this *Regis* thing?"

"We will abandon the business of patient waiting for what we can pick up and grab the girl and the mob holding her prisoner. When they are disposed of, we'll take a plane and go out to look into this *Regis* business."

Monk sighed. "That means the mob will learn that Doc Savage is not really dead."

"Not necessarily," said Doc Savage, his remarkable voice still expressionless.

DOC SAVAGE listened for a time at the headset connected to the dictagraph microphone. There was nothing interesting.

"They do not talk much at this time of the afternoon," the bronze man said. "We might as well close in on them."

He switched off the eavesdropping device, and preceded Monk and Ham through the door. They climbed stairs.

Monk said, "If the public learns you aren't dead, it's going to create a sensation."

"Nobody is going to understand why you did it," Ham added.

Doc Savage spoke quietly.

"That the bomb sent to our headquarters did not kill me was due simply to the precaution that moved me to withdraw to the library and turn the X-ray apparatus on by remote control," he said. "Whoever sent that bomb had reasoned the package would be X-rayed, and had connected an electroscopic device of some sort in the package, hooking it to a detonator."

Monk agreed, "Yeah. And then you fixed up that wax image and got the police to let the idea get out that you were dead. Only I don't see yet why such elaborate preparation was necessary."

"Whoever thought of providing against the bomb being X-rayed was clever," Doc Savage explained. "No simple trick would have fooled that person. That the would-be killer should think the death trap had succeeded was convenient for the simple reason that no more attempts would be made on my life, leaving me free to make an investigation unhampered."

"Um-m-m," said Monk. "I'd still like to know what is behind all of this mystery."

Doc Savage did not reply. Instead, the bronze man went up a particularly narrow flight of steps, poking the beam of a flashlight ahead of him. He reached an overhead trapdoor.

A shove caused this to open silently. They climbed out

upon a flat roof top which was comparatively private, because it was surrounded by a high parapet.

The roof top was crisscrossed by a web of wires, apparently portions of radio aërials. This was nothing to attract attention, there hardly being a roof top in Manhattan which was not so cluttered.

Doc Savage drew a pair of pliers from a pocket and calmly cut one of the apparent aërial wires.

Ham muttered, "I hope that works!"

"It will!" Monk grunted. "I made the plant and hook-up myself."

"That," flipped Ham, "is why I have some doubts."

Monk snorted indignantly. "Listen, shyster! That was fixed up three days ago. Cutting that wire causes a relay to open in the basement of that house where the mob is hanging out. The opening relay closes an electrical contact which starts a phonograph loudspeaker—there it is! Fan your ears out and listen!"

It was hardly necessary for ears to be fanned out to catch the sounds which were now coming from the lower part of the building. First, there was a series of great crashes, as of wooden doors being burst inward; then came a great yell.

"Police raid!" thundered a great voice. "Watch the back and front doors!"

In the shelter of the roof coaming, Monk chuckled.

"Believe it or not, that's *my* voice," he said. "Boy, would I make an actor!"

"Come," Doc Savage said.

THEY were on the adjacent roof by now, and, looking about, they had no difficulty discerning a roof hatch. Doc Savage had scouted the layout previously. To the left of the roof hatch was a bank of chimneys which offered excellent concealment. Doc and his aides crouched behind these.

The bronze man produced, from inside his clothing, a small object which might have been a cigarette case, except that he never used tobacco. There was a round button on the edge of the case. He rested a metallic thumb against the button and pointed the case at the roof hatch.

The loud-speaker device was still rapping orders downstairs. A police siren whine came from the contrivance. A coarse voice exhorted speed, caution.

"*Sh-h-h!*" Monk breathed. "Here they come!"

The roof hatch flew open. A man popped out. He was a stocky, questionable-looking fellow, was wearing a scared expression. He started across the roof top, as if his sole idea was to get to some other roof, from which they evidently had an avenue of escape ready.

A very sharp ear might have caught the small sound from the case which Doc Savage held.

The runner grunted loudly, stopped, looked about vacantly, then laid himself down on the roof top.

Another man appeared. He was calmer. Turning, he spoke to some one below.

"Take it easy, Miss Crale," he said. "There's not a chance of them grabbing us."

Velma Crale's voice said, "Well it *would* be too bad if the police busted up the thing at this point."

Velma Crale then came into view. Three men followed her. The young woman was not bound, gagged, nor in any way confined to indicate she was a prisoner. In fact, she seemed perfectly free, and as anxious as the others to leave the vicinity with speed.

"I wonder how on earth the cops found us?" she snapped angrily.

The small object in Doc Savage's hand made several of its small noises. Velma Crale's companions made gasping noises and sank into immobility. As the last was going down, the young woman comprehended what was happening.

"Darts!" she snapped, and tried to run.

Leaving the concealment of the bank of chimneys, Doc Savage overhauled her. She fought him briskly for a moment after his hands were on her, but saw the futility of that, and gave up.

"It looks," she said, "like I've got myself in a pickle."

MONK and Ham were examining the men who had gone down, making sure each was senseless, and also extracting the tiny darts which Doc Savage had expelled with the pneumatic gun which resembled a cigarette case.

The darts were fashioned like hypodermic needles and

eost almost five dollars apiece to have made. They were, therefore, worth saving.

Ham came over and confronted the girl.

"You are what might be called a smooth female," he said bitingly.

She frowned at him innocently. "What do you mean?"

"We figured you were a prisoner," Ham snapped. "Now it appears you are one of the mob."

"Oh, my," said the young woman. "You believe what you see, don't you?"

"That comedy does not get across," Ham retorted.

The young woman ignored him, and studied Doc Savage. The bronze man's features were absolutely expressionless, and the young woman did not seem reassured.

"I was a prisoner," she said, earnestly, "but they turned me loose. They would rather have me escape from them than to fall into the hands of the police."

Ham snorted loudly, skeptically, in a manner which plainly called Velma Crale a liar. She kicked at Ham, but Doc Savage, holding her, tilted her off balance, and she missed. She tried to kick Doc, to bite him. She had no luck.

Doc Savage suggested, "Maybe you had better tell us the motive behind this trouble, if you don't mind."

She looked at him, then put back her head, mouth open. Her laughter was like the crash of a pile of dishes.

"And lose more money than Rockefeller ever saw?" she jeered. "Mrs. Crale didn't raise no daughters that silly!"

Ham remarked, "We're going to have to give this young lady the works, it seems." He twirled his cane vigorously.

Velma Crale sobered. She eyed them.

"You'll have a tough time," she said.

Doc Savage lifted her, carried her easily, despite her most violent struggles, and made his way across the roof to the house where he had been eavesdropping, and out of the front door.

His two aides, Monk and Ham, brought the senseless men. They loaded them into the machine which was painted and equipped to resemble a taxicab.

"Keep the girl here," Doc Savage told Monk and Ham.

Doc himself went into the house, to the roof, and

down into the dwelling which had been the mob's hangout. He found a miserably furnished place which smelled of stale tobacco smoke and overcooked food. He searched.

There seemed to be nothing but fingerprints. Doc did not trouble to photograph these, but merely powdered them, and studied them at length—fixing the classification of the whorls in his trained memory so that, if he saw them later, he would remember them.

Remembering the fingerprints was not the difficult task it seemed, at first. It was merely a case of fixing mentally the code letters indicating the classification of the prints.

Doc went back and joined his two aides, Velma Crale, and the senseless men.

"Where to?" asked Monk, who was at the wheel.

"Headquarters," Doc Savage said. "We'll question this crowd."

"But how about the *Regis?*" Ham wanted to know.

"The questioning will not take long," Doc told him. "Then we'll fly out to the liner."

They entered the skyscraper by the basement garage, existence of which was known to very few, and from thence upward by a special speed elevator which had been put out of commission by the explosion, and later repaired. Thus, no one saw them gain the eighty-sixth floor of the skyscraper.

Doc Savage unlocked the metal door which admitted them to the reception room. This door was undamaged, although, at the end of one corridor nearest the laboratory, there was a barrier of planks, closing an aperture where the wall had been blown down.

Doc Savage and his aides carried their prisoners into the reception room, which was furnished only with a huge safe, an inlaid table and a number of comfortably upholstered chairs.

Ham looked around, puzzled.

"I wonder where Long Tom is?" he remarked.

Monk also began to register uneasy curiosity. Major Thomas J. "Long Tom" Roberts was the fifth member of Doc Savage's group of five aides. Long Tom was the physical weakling of the crowd, thin, not very tall, and with a none-too-healthy-appearing skin. He was a wizard with electricity.

He was supposed to be here, keeping an eye on the priceless equipment of the headquarters, to see that vandals or souvenir hunters did not carry things off.

"Long Tom!" Monk whooped.

Doc Savage moved suddenly, shoving Monk and Ham violently. They sprawled on through the door into the library, leaving the prisoners deposited on the reception-room floor.

Monk rolled over, mouth coming open to ask questions. But he did not ask. There was no need.

Grimly, businesslike men with rifles were coming up the stairs and out of two elevators.

Chapter VII

SEA ENIGMA

DOC SAVAGE, when doing his best, could move with a speed equaled by few living humans. He used some of that speed now, making for the door.

But one of the mob in the corridor had thoughtfully provided himself with a heavy chair which could be used as a weapon, a tool for demolishing doors, or, as in the present instance, an object wherewith to keep doors from being slammed. He managed to toss the chair accurately, so that it held the door open. The next instant, the men outside hit the door.

Doc Savage, braced against the other side of the door, managed to hold it.

"Get your machine pistols!" he rapped at Monk and Ham.

These two came out of the library, dragging from under their clothing weapons which resembled oversize automatic pistols, equipped with spiral drum magazines.

A coldly determined voice on the other side of the door spoke.

"If you guys know what's good for you, come out of there without any funny business!"

"Hah!" the homely Monk jeered loudly. "Watch us!"

The man outside said, *"Watch this!"*

Something about the fellow's tone caused Doc Savage and his two aides to want very much to see what was in the corridor. Doc gestured.

Monk ran to a briefcase which belonged to Ham, opened it and dug out a small mirror which the vain Ham carried. They used this to get a glimpse outside. The door itself was of bulletproof steel, so they were safe from lead as long as they kept behind it.

"Blazes!" Monk gurgled.

ALL three of them could see what the mob outside had wanted them to see—a pale-faced man.

The man was bound and gagged, and a knife was being brandished before his face, but that did not account for his paleness. His was a natural pallor.

He looked unhealthy, as if he had spent his entire life in some one's mushroom cellar. He was, furthermore, underweight, and there was no healthy amount of color in his hair and eyes.

"Long Tom!" Monk gulped.

"Exactly!" snapped the man outside. "The other member of your crowd! Watch what that knife does to him!"

"Wait!" Doc Savage rapped.

There was a startling power to the bronze man's single word—an arresting quality that seemed impossible for a mere vocal tone to possess.

"If we surrender, will you guarantee Long Tom will not be touched?" the bronze man continued.

"That's just what we were getting at," growled one of the men outside.

Doc Savage's flake gold eyes drifted over Monk and Ham, who looked very uneasy.

"Take it easy," Doc said, and opened the door.

The men with the rifles advanced. They were elated, none too cautious. In a compact body, they came through the door. One man remained behind, gripping the puny-looking Long Tom.

Doc Savage retreated before the men as they entered

the office. The bronze man's hands were in the air; his attitude was one of complete surrender.

Derek Flammen, bony hands clenching a revolver, his ponylike face alight with nervous triumph, appeared in the hallway.

"This is wonderful!" he chortled. "This is what I really call progress!"

Doc SAVAGE stopped. He spoke, and there was something in the crispness of his voice, the power of it, that arrested developments for the moment.

"You engineered this?" the bronze man asked Flammen.

Derek Flammen wet his lips, seeming nervous.

"Exactly," he said. "And I would advise you to try nothing queer!"

Doc Savage asked, "Flammen, just what is your connection with this affair?"

Derek Flammen answered promptly and levelly.

"I was involved innocently, at first, not knowing what it was all about," he snapped. "Since then, I have learned some things. I still do not know what is behind this. But I do know that a great many millions of dollars and a number of lives are involved. That money interests me. Indeed it does. If any one gets hold of that wealth, it is going to be Derek Flammen."

The girl, Velma Crale spoke up sarcastically.

"Some one is going to get disappointed in this game of snatch-grab!" she snapped.

"Let us hope," Doc Savage said, quietly, "that is correct."

The bronze man casually continued his retreat. He seemed to pay no particular attention to where he went, but he stepped heavily on certain parts of the reception room rug.

There was an abrupt *swish* of mechanism. Something seemed to flash in mid-air between the bronze man and the advancing mob.

Derek Flammen's men stopped as if they had run into something invisible. They began to curse.

"There's some kind of plate-glass wall dropped down!" a man squawled.

Instantly, confusion descended. Guns whooped, and bullets flattened weirdly on the glass, which in turn cracked slightly in places, but did not break.

Long Tom, the puny-looking prisoner out in the corridor, began to squawl something. His words did not at first penetrate the din.

"Behind you!" he yelled. "More men hidden in the laboratory!"

Doc Savage read the thin electrical wizard's lips, spun. He was a bit tardy. Men were coming out of the library and laboratory. They had rifles. Plainly, they intended to shoot.

The ceiling of the reception room, which to the eye appeared to be an ordinary ceiling neatly ornamented with modernistic strips of metal, was actually quite a remarkable ceiling.

Past attempts on his life had moved Doc Savage to install the descending sheets of bulletproof glass, which could be dropped with great speed by the application of pressure on certain spots in the floor. Other sheets protected the center of the reception room from the library door. Doc now dropped these panels.

But the attackers were not without means of coping with the unusual defense. They produced explosive grenades, plucked the firing pins, and heaved them. The first opened with a detonation that threatened to complete the demolition of the skyscraper's top.

Other grenades landed. They were loaded with some modern explosive which detonated with an eye-hurting white flash. The blasts set the ears ringing, made it impossible to hear other sounds. The glass plates collapsed. Bullets came storming in.

Doc Savage and his aides were outnumbered several times by heavily armed and prepared men.

DUE to the perilous nature of the peculiar work which he was following, Doc Savage habitually made use of every conceivable precautionary measure. Otherwise, he would have long ago lost his life. This skyscraper headquarters was a mechanical labyrinth.

In it was every defensive measure which the man of bronze had been able to devise. In the high aerie, he was as safe from would-be killers as he was anywhere else on earth.

The place was a maze of hidden recesses, runways and concealed doors. The bronze man made gestures, indicating that Monk and Ham should position themselves close to him. They did so. The bronze man stooped, and his fists rapped sharply at different portions of the floor.

There was a loud report—sharper than the blast of the grenades. It was accompanied by a flash of white light infinitely more intense than that from a photographer's flash gun. Moreover, this flash had some peculiar quality which caused it to blind all completely for a moment.

There ensued an interval of fully ten seconds when none of the raiders could see a thing except queer lights in their eyeballs. During that time, there was some rapid moving about and a lot of cursing.

A man got his vision back and immediately saw that Long Tom, the puny-looking electrical wizard, had vanished from the corridor. That was not even the start of it. Doc Savage, Monk and Ham were gone.

In the ensuing confusion, the girl, Velma Crale, got herself untied and made a break. They shot at her, but she ducked into the stairway and made good her escape.

Derek Flammen suddenly lost his nerve.

"Beat it, guys!" he yelled, and set an example.

They had the elevators waiting, the operators cowed by guns held in the hands of more of Flammen's men. Cramming themselves into the cages, the raiders descended.

Once on the lobby level, Derek Flammen showed that he could think quickly. He had two of his armed aides force themselves into the basement switchboard room and cut off all electrical power from the building. The elevators immediately became inactive, with one exception.

The exception was Doc Savage's speed elevator. Power for this came from the bronze man's private electrical system, with an automatic generating room deep in the basement.

But sometime during the excitement, the raiders had taken care of the speed elevator. Fortunately, Doc Savage discovered it in time. He stopped his men, on the verge of entering, with an outstretched arm.

"Don't use it!" he warned.

"Huh!" Monk exploded. "I don't see nothin' wrong?"

The bronze man pointed out that the electric bulb which ordinarily illuminated the cage had been smashed, leaving comparative murk inside. The reason for this, they soon discovered: a parcel of high explosive and an electric detonator, the latter attached to the elevator control so that, had the control been moved in haste, the blast would have been set off.

"Blazes!" complained Monk. "They're gonna get away!"

They did.

THAT the raiders and the young woman, Velma Crale, had entirely escaped became clear in the course of the next ten minutes. There was no sign of them down on the street.

Returning to the eighty-sixth floor headquarters, Doc Savage went over the floor to make sure none of the trapdoors—giving access to crawl-ways beneath—had been left open. He did not want casual visitors to discover them. They had all closed. He reloaded the flash device with the powder that burned with such blinding qualities.

"Long Tom," the bronze man suggested, "you stick here."

The feeble-looking Long Tom grinned sourly. "O. K."

He had visions of missing out on future developments by being left behind.

"Be careful," Doc warned. "Don't let them get hold of you again."

"Sure," Long Tom agreed, cheerfully. "They wouldn't have gotten me before, only they said they were building inspectors, and showed badges to prove it. They must have stolen or faked the badges. Anyway, first thing I knew, they had me."

Doc Savage did not advise more caution in the future. It was not often that Long Tom got taken in.

Accompanied by Monk and Ham, the bronze man left the huge building which housed his headquarters. They drove, in an innocent-looking armored sedan, toward the Hudson River water front, where Doc Savage maintained secretly a huge hangar housing a number of boats and aircraft. The hangar masqueraded as a warehouse owned by a mythical Hidalgo Trading Co.

Monk sighed loudly and said, "I don't make heads or tails of this!" in a baffled tone.

"I am beginning to get some pretty good ideas," said the dapper Ham.

"Yeah?" Monk snorted.

"There are at least three mobs fighting to get hold of something," Ham said. "The girl, Velma Crale, is heading one crowd. Derek Flammen is heading another. And the third is bossed by person or persons unknown."

Monk sniffed in the insulting manner which he always used to greet any suggestion made by Ham.

"Suppose you know what they're fighting over?" he demanded.

Ham scowled at Monk, became suddenly indignant, and yelled, "You awful mistake of nature! I don't know, but I'll bet my guess is better——"

"We'll take the big speed plane for the flight to the *Regis,*" interrupted Doc Savage.

Chapter VIII

HORROR AFLOAT

SOMETHING over an hour had by this time elapsed since the mysterious, unfinished S O S had come from the liner *Regis.* Several steamers were enroute toward the spot, but these craft were not making much headway. The reason for this was a violent storm which had sprung up.

The arising of the storm was inexplicable. The weather bureau charts showed a uniform area of high pressure over that section of the Atlantic, together with no conditions indicating a change.

Yet there was a storm. It was mostly wind, although there was also a light rain, together with some thunder and lightning. Radio reports from the ships rushing to the

Regis indicated the force of wind was increasing. Already, it had attained almost the velocity of a full gale.

Two U.S. coast guard planes which had started to fly to the *Regis* found themselves buffeted about badly. A number of news reel planes and newspaper photographic planes were likewise beset. It began to seem as if they would have to turn back.

As homely Monk put it, "Brother, if this zephyr got hold of a man's hair, it'd sure scalp 'im!"

Ham, the dapper lawyer, said nothing. Ham had become somewhat greenish-looking. He was airsick, something that rarely befell him. But then, air as rough as this was rarely encountered.

Sprawled beside Ham, hanging onto an arm-rest with a ghastly grim intentness, was the dapper lawyer's rather weird-looking pet, Chemistry. In some respects, Chemistry looked remarkably human. Certain it was that Chemistry bore a startling likeness to the homely chemist, Monk—which was probably the reason why Ham had adopted Chemistry as a pet.

Chemistry was some species of South American monkey, although it was true no one had ever been able to decide just what species. He was airsick also.

Across the plane aisle, balancing easily with the plane's antics, big ears fanned out as if to aid in flying, if such should become necessary, sat Monk's pet, Habeas Corpus, the pig. Habeas was an Arabian hog, composed of, other than ears, nothing much except legs and an inquisitive snout.

Monk and Ham rarely went anywhere without these two pets, and it was significant that Habeas Corpus and Chemistry got along about as well as did Monk and Ham. Periodically, they had to be forcibly restrained from eating each other alive.

The big plane leaped, heaved, and all but did a loop. Doc Savage fought the controls. The radio receivers inside his helmet—he was using the headset rather than the loud-speaker because of the bad ether conditions—were a bedlam of static. He had just managed to pick up a fragmentary message indicating that the coast guard and news reel planes had been forced to turn back.

This big ship of Doc Savage's was an all-metal, low-wing job with three motors. Streamlining had been carried out to an infinite degree. The plane, as a matter of fact, was perhaps the fastest and most stanch craft of its size in existence.

Monk howled cheerfully, "Anything on the radio from the *Regis,* Doc?"

"No," Doc Savage said.

The plane's cabin was efficiently soundproof, so that it was comparatively quiet inside.

"In this case, no news is bad news," Monk declared.

"Will you shut up, you human period!" Ham gritted. "Just the sound of your voice makes my ears ache!"

Monk began to squeak a sea chantey having to do with men who died at sea and had their bones picked by sharks, managing in some inexplicable fashion to keep time to the pitching of the gale-buffeted plane.

THE *Regis* lay in the trough of the sea, taking the short, violent waves as they came. At times, water sheeted almost completely over her decks. Brine and rain wetted her down from bow to stern. Smoke came from her funnels, but the screws did not seem to be turning over. She was a stout, new hooker, this *Regis,* however. Little likelihood of her leaking as yet.

"What I wanta know," Monk grumbled, "is how we're gonna get aboard?"

They had picked up the liner without a great deal of difficulty.

Doc Savage offered no suggestion about how they were to get aboard until he had sent the big plane in two slow spirals about the liner, barely clearing the mast tops.

"Have to use parachutes," he said. "One of you will remain in the plane and pick us up later, if it can be done."

Monk peered downward, muttered, "I see a few bodies on deck."

This was true. Here and there was a prone form, most of them lodged against obstructions, where they had been washed by the waves, or tumbled by the pitch of the boat.

"Who's gonna stick with the plane?" Monk demanded.

"You are," Ham said, arousing slightly from his illness.

"Like heck!"

"Match for it," Doc suggested.

Monk promptly produced a coin, said, "Call it!"

"Heads," groaned Ham.

Monk smothered a grin, flipped, and Ham naturally lost, since the coin was one with tails on both sides. Monk had carried it for some time, hoping for a chance to trim the dapper Ham.

Grinning from ear to ear, the homely chemist buckled on a parachute while Ham took over the controls glumly.

"That boat is probably jumping around worse than this plane," Ham consoled himself sourly.

The parachute descent to the decks of the *Regis* was accomplished with no great difficulty. Cold calculation robbed it of most of its dangers. Doc Savage dropped a smoke bomb first to get the wind's direction and velocity. Then he had Monk bail out.

His purpose in sending Monk down first was to have himself in a position to offer assistance, should it be necessary.

Monk landed on the after deck. By a wild scramble, he managed to escape from the harness before the wind carried the silken 'chute lobe overboard.

Monk was still wearing a queer look from the narrowness of his escape when Doc Savage landed expertly near by. The bronze man was already out of the harness and let it go instantly.

Together, they walked across the deck toward the amidships sector. They began to notice strange things almost at once.

"Hey!" Monk exploded. "Look how sunburned this fellow is!"

THE homely chemist was indicating the first of the bodies. The victim was a large man, whose skin was burned a beet red. Doc Savage went over and made a hasty examination. When he stood erect, he shook his head.

"Life extinct," he said. "The cause is not plain. It is unfortunate that we did not bring certain instruments and apparatus for a chemical analysis and diagnosis."

"The guy is dead," Monk muttered. "Speaking roughly, what'd you say ailed him?"

"Roughly," Doc Savage said, "the man appears to have died of sunstroke."

Monk scratched his head, and they walked on. They found two more motionless forms, both without life. Nearing the salon companionway, Monk paid particular attention to the seams of the deck. The deck planking was of teakwood, with compound in the seams, and some of this compound apparently had been squeezed out.

"Blazes!" Monk squawked. "Doc, you remember that silver sloop which was found on Long Island Sound with all of those dead people aboard?"

"Very distinctly," the bronze man admitted. "Exactly such conditions as these were found aboard."

They entered the salon, and it became evident that death was far from general aboard. The salon, which extended the full beam of the ship and was equipped with comfortable chairs and divans, had been converted into an emergency hospital. Evidently no lookout was being kept, and the howl of the gale must have drowned the sound of the plane's motors, which were silenced.

Suddenly, it became plain why no watch was being kept. The eyes of those present, for the most part, were covered with bandages.

A man approached Doc Savage and Monk. He was a lean fellow with stringy muscles and a leathery hide somewhat less sunburned than the others—if it was sunburn. He lifted a corner of the bandage covering his eyes.

"Who are you gentlemen?" he demanded. "And how in all damnation did you escape that infernal heat?"

Doc Savage made known the identity of himself and Monk.

The stringy man was properly astounded at the information. He stripped the bandage from his eyes, as if to see more of the newcomers, only to blink violently and replace the wrapper.

"This has been an incredible thing!" he gasped. "My name is Ward. I am one of the stewards. Can I give you any information?"

"The whole story," Doc Savage said.

The man told about the strange heat, the actions of the passengers and the crew.

"It grew worse and worse," he said. "The heat, I mean.

There came a time when, I think, every one aboard this ship was overcome. And then it went away."

"How long did it require for the return of normal temperatures?" Doc Savage asked.

"Some time," said the man. "In fact, it is still warm. But the strange *heat*—the stuff that knocked every one out—why, that disappeared almost instantly."

"Have you seen any sign of a man named Thurston H. Wardhouse?" Doc Savage asked.

"No," said the man.

"Or of my two aides, Renny and Johnny?"

"They were aboard," the other admitted. "But there has been so sign of them since that—that period when the fantastic heat had every one unconscious."

Doc Savage said nothing to Monk about being worried, but the homely chemist could detect perturbation in the haste with which his bronze chief pushed a search of the *Regis*. They took the steward, who had said his name was Ward, along to serve as guide in the hunt for Renny, Johnny and Thurston H. Wardhouse.

Searching an ocean liner is not a task lightly dismissed. When the scrutinizing is delegated to three individuals, the passages and cabins of such a vessel assume the characteristics of a vast labyrinth.

They made a number of discoveries.

First, the magnetism seemed to be gone out of the magnetic compasses.

"It was the same way on that silver sloop in Long Island Sound!" Monk reminded.

Secondly, they concluded that those individuals who had been deepest in the innards of the liner throughout the spell of queer heat had been least affected. The firemen in the engine room, for instance, while they had perspired prodigiously, had not been overcome in numbers.

They did not find Johnny, Renny, or the mysterious Thurston H. Wardhouse.

An hour later, Doc Savage announced a decision.

"It would take a week to search the ship thoroughly," he said. "Renny and Johnny should have answered, since we have been shouting their names. They are either incapacitated, or not aboard."

"If they're not aboard, where the blazes did they go?" Monk wanted to know immediately.

Instead of answering, Doc Savage said, "To make a thorough investigation in an effort to learn just what happened on this ship, we will need some highly specialized apparatus. That mysterious heat seems to be the really baffling angle, and it is essential that we get an idea of what it is.

"It might be best, therefore, to radio Long Tom to fly out with some equipment. That would be quicker than sending Ham back for it."

Monk was peering upward. He could see their plane swinging in idle circles overhead, such sounds as its three motors made completely lost in the howl of the gale.

"Uh-huh," he said, absently.

"We will learn whether the radio equipment can be operated," Doc added.

Their handy man, Ward, accompanied them to the radio shack, which was really not a shack but quite a palatial cubbyhole of marble and mahogany. Ward's vision seemed to be improving.

"I was lucky enough to remain below decks throughout the strange heat," he said. "As a matter of fact, they had me peeling potatoes. From now on, I shall never hate potato peeling."

THE radio equipment was of the most modern type. Doc Savage examined it swiftly, then gave his attention to the operators. The men were dead.

There was no sign of Renny or Johnny in the radio room.

Unexpectedly, a strange sound became audible. It was a small, eerie trilling with a quality of a heterodyning electric circuit. It ran up and down the musical scale eerily, and caused the man Ward to peer at the apparatus curiously.

"First time I ever heard a radio make a noise like that," he growled.

Doc Savage said nothing. Nor did Monk volunteer the truth—that the trilling noise was a small, unconscious thing which Doc Savage did in moments of stress. In the present case, it meant that the bronze man had found something interesting. He pointed it out.

"Some one was evidently seated at the key and collapsed, upsetting a bottle of ink," he said. "Notice the print of a hand inked on the floor?"

Monk looked, casually at first, then with a shocked intentness. The print of the hand was so huge that it could have been made by only one person.

"Blazes!" he barked shrilly. "Renny!"

"Exactly."

"But what became of 'im?"

Doc Savage did not reply immediately, but moved about the radio room. On the parqueted floor, near the door, he noted a smear of ink.

"Made by a dragging hand," he said. "Renny seems to have been carried out shortly after he collapsed. At any rate, the ink on his hands had not had time to dry."

The bronze man went to the radio apparatus. The next few moments he spent in solving the controls and sending the call letters and relay combination of his own receiving station atop the skyscraper.

The station had not been disabled by the explosions. The relay combination—it was an adaptation of the device in use in land line telegraph relay stations—evidently sent the buzzer into operation in the New York station, the receiving side of which was kept always on the air.

AN answer came in Morse code. There was still a bit too much static for effective voice transmission and reception. The "fist" of the sender was crisp, efficient. Doc identified it immediately. Long Tom.

"Get from the storehouse equipment cases numbers 14, 73, 21, 22, 23, and 86," Doc Savage transmitted. *"Load them in one of the planes and get them out to the liner Regis."*

The bronze man gave the numbers of the equipment cases from memory, knowing that they held devices for scientific analysis.

"O.K." Tom tapped back.

"Anything new there?" Doc queried over the air.

"Nothing," replied the electrical wizard. *"The police*

and newspapermen did a bit of investigating, but they are not here now. They asked a lot of questions about whether you were really dead. At least, the newspapermen did. And the police wanted to know what had become of you."

"When will you be out?" Doc Savage asked.

"Very shortly," Tom replied.

Doc Savage switched off the radio transmitter. He turned to go.

Monk glanced about curiously.

"Where'd our friend Ward go?" he pondered aloud.

Ward, the helpful steward, was nowhere in sight.

"Probably he didn't want to stick his nose into our private business," Monk decided.

Monk and Doc Savage went out to continue their search for Johnny and Renny, and to await the arrival of Long Tom by plane from New York with the equipment.

Ward, the useful steward, watched them furtively from behind a ventilator down the deck. Ward's face had a vicious, animallike look.

"A swell break for your Uncle Rastus!" he gritted cheerfully.

Chapter IX

SEA DECOY

WARD made no effort to follow Doc Savage and Monk. Instead, the fellow waited until the two were out of sight, then scuddled for the radio shack door, the wind popping his coat tails on his hips. He shut the door behind him and made sure the spring lock had sprung.

He went to the radio apparatus. The fist with which he tapped out call letters was plain, good; his hand on the dials was skillful. He used a very short wave on the special short-wave transmitter and receiver layout. He got his party very shortly.

The other operator had a slow, draggy fist, with a good many combinations. It sounded as if the fellow was purposefully trying to disguise his sending.

"*Doc Savage and Monk are aboard,*" said Ward. "*It's damned lucky I was here. They're having Long Tom come out from New York. I thought we might do something about that.*"

"*We might,*" agreed the distant radio man. "*Hold your hat a minute. I'll see what old Glass Eyes says.*"

The wait was not extensive.

"*Get hold of Long Tom and have him fly due south-southeast from Montauk lightship,*" directed the radio man with the slow fist. "*Instruct him to land when he sights us, and we'll take care of him.*"

"*O.K.*"

The hook-up with the other station was about to be broken by Ward when the distant operator interrupted with a hurried series of dots.

"*Hold it,*" he instructed. "*Old Glass Eyes has just thought up another of them really titanic ideas he goes in for.*"

There followed several moments of earnest instructions. Ward, the self-designed steward, listened intently to the dots and dashes as they came through the interference of static.

"*Ha, ha!*" he tapped when they had ended. "*O.K.*"

He now hurriedly changed the wave length of the set, putting it on the frequency which Doc Savage had used to communicate with Long Tom. The man must have eavesdropped and learned the call letters of Doc Savage's New York headquarters station, because he tapped the letters out rapidly, together with the combination of the relay call device.

An anxious expression on the man's face cleared when Long Tom's crisp fist answered. The fellow had been afraid Long Tom had already left.

Long Tom asked over the air, "*What is it?*"

"*Your instructions are changed,*" tapped the man at the *Regis* key.

"*Hey!*" Long Tom broke in. "*You are not Doc!*"

"*This is Monk,*" transmitted the self-designated steward. *"I fell down on the dang deck and twisted my wrist, so you may not be able to read this."*

"Go ahead," tapped Long Tom, completely deceived. *"What are my altered instructions?"*

"Fly south-southeast from Montauk lightship," directed the other. *"Pick up a searchlight blinking the letters DOC over and over again, and land on the sea to be picked up. Don't be too surprised by the appearance of the vessel from which the signal will be blinked."*

"What has happened?" Long Tom tapped inquisitively.

The other man made several exclamation points with his key.

"Plenty!" he transmitted. *"No time to give the details to you now. We'll tell you when you land. Don't come to the Regis, because Doc and me won't be aboard. If it's any consolation, I think we've about got this mystery cleared up. And now, 73's."*

"73's," Long Tom replied.

The terminology *"73"* is used by telegraphers and newspapermen to convey a wish that future good fortune may attend the other. The man who had given himself the name of Ward laughed harshly after he had sent it.

WARD'S work at the key was not done when he had ended his communication with Long Tom. The man shut off the short-wave apparatus, and cut in one of the other sets which operated on the longer wave lengths.

He got ready to send, but did not do so immediately. He sat there wearing a concentrated expression, plotting out what he was to transmit. Then he thumbed the sending "bug" vigorously.

"S O S," he transmitted frantically. *"Doc Savage alive, responsible for attack on liner Regis! Is murdering many people!"*

The man added the call letters of the liner *Regis*, and hammered a few more frantic S O S signals. This was to give the effect of utter terror.

"Doc Savage killing people on Regis with strange machine!" he continued. *"Send help! Doc Savage——"*

He broke it off there with a steady pressure against the "dot" side of the "bug," an expedient which caused a steady stream of dots to go out and end in a closed circuit which transmitted a steady, continuous wave whine. It would sound very much as if the sender had died at his post.

To make the indication of murder more effective, the man who had claimed to be a steward grasped one of the dead radio operators, heaved and got the fellow into a chair before the key.

One of the dead man's fingers was inserted in the upset ink, in which had been left the print of Renny's huge hand. The inked finger described a fragmentary message:

DOC SAVAGE DID——

He smeared the last, as if the printing finger had completely lost its strength before the missive could be completed.

Stepping back, the man surveyed his handiwork. He made a few minor changes in the position of the body, after which he grinned his satisfaction, and left the radio room. He peered upward as he worked along the deck.

Doc Savage's plane, Ham at the controls, was nowhere in sight above. The man listened. He could not pick up the sound of the motor.

"I hope to hell his wings came off, or something!" the man grated.

He found Doc Savage and Monk.

"The wind seems to be dying down," he said.

"That oughta make it simpler for Long Tom to get out here," vouchsafed the homely Monk. "Reckon Long Tom is in the air by now."

As a matter of fact, Long Tom was not quite in the air, but he was out on the Hudson River in the rather small, low-wing seaplane which he had chosen for the flight.

The craft was a staunch one, and not an amphibian; therefore, it was very stable for descending and arising from the sea. The motor was a huge thing which could literally yank the craft off the top of a wave into the air. The big engine did its most spectacular work now, and the plane moaned up into the murk above New York City. It headed east.

Long Tom missed, by not more than fifteen minutes,

the extra editions of the newspapers which hit the stands announcing that a new S O S had come from the *Regis*.

Doc Savage was involved! Doc Savage was alive! The S O S had said he was responsible for killings aboard the *Regis!*

The newspapers broke out type so big that it had not been used in years.

A score of photographic, newspaper and coast guard planes took the air, determined to reach the *Regis*. The mysterious gale which had lashed up so unexpectedly was dying now, anyway.

Long Tom flew out to sea blissfully ignorant of anything out of the way. He kept his radio apparatus tuned on the wave length used by Doc Savage and his aides in communicating with each other, so he did not hear any of the emergency news broadcasts about Doc Savage attacking the liner.

There was a haze off the end of Long Island, but Long Tom had no difficulty picking up Montauk lightship, because Montauk was a radio beacon, and could be flown to easily by use of the directional radio which the plane carried. From the lightship, the electrical wizard set his course south-southeast, as he had been directed.

That the radio directions might have been spurious did not occur to him. He never gave it a thought. He used a pair of binoculars with wide fields and swept the sea.

He knew he was flying to a point well south of the liner *Regis,* but he did not give that a thought. He wanted to sight a light signaling "DOC." He concentrated on that.

After a time, he saw it. It was a very powerful light, and he knew it must be on a craft of rather considerable size. It was rather dark, there being no moon; there were no clouds.

Long Tom circled the blinking light. It turned upward and found his plane. This blinded him so that he could not see a thing below.

"I'll give 'em some of their own medicine," grunted the puny-looking electrical wizard.

He dropped a parachute flare. The white light spraying from this showed him what was below. He hung out of the cabin window. His mouth came open. He was astounded.

He thought, at first, that he was looking at a long, bright rock. Then he knew differently, because the charts showed some hundreds of fathoms of water in this vicinity. And no rock could be that shiny.

The thing was long, narrow, tapered at front and back, was convex, and made him think of half of a big metal cigar floating on the water.

"Dirigible!" he exploded.

He flew down, intending to land before the parachute flare dunked itself into the sea. The plane came down with a whistle, for it was fast on the response. He straightened out to land.

Then he saw it was no dirigible floating on the water. It was something else. He goggled. He had never seen anything like it before, and could not even guess what it might be.

He stared so hard that he made a very bad landing. The plane hit a wave, bounced, heeled over. Long Tom was sure it would capsize.

THE plane did not capsize, due to the stability of its construction rather than any superhuman flying on Long Tom's part. It did all but bury itself in the sea. Long Tom cut the engine and wiped imaginary sweat drops off his overly huge forehead.

The searchlight splashed fairly into his eyes when he stuck his head and shoulders out of the escape hatch in the roof of the plane. He shielded his eyes with an arm and waved for them to take the light away. They did not take it away. The light seemed to be coming closer.

"Doc must have a bunch of greenhorns helping him!" Long Tom complained, and ducked back in the cabin to get another flare. They were constructed so he could hold them in a hand and burn them.

He shoved out of the cabin again. His mouth fell open. The searchlight had approached much more rapidly than he had expected. It was almost upon him.

Water sloshed, hissed, sobbed. A great hulk loomed. The weird, shiny craft! He could see the fantastic brightness of it, even in the darkness. It was almost upon him. It *was* on him!

The jar as the thing hit the plane came an instant after

Long Tom flung himself flat and grasped a generator propeller, the only protuberance handy. The ship skewered around. It tilted. A wing went under. Then the whole was submerged.

Long Tom was carried down. Water tore at him. Then he was caught between the side of the fantastic thing of the sea and the hull of the plane. The impact was terrific, and air left Long Tom's lungs.

He was not in a condition to think of many things. But he knew suddenly that Doc Savage was not here, that he had been tricked.

He had a horrible feeling that the sea was a million miles deep, that he was at the bottom of it, and could never get to the top again. Then he did not feel anything, or think any more about Doc Savage and tricks.

Chapter X

UNCLE PENGUIN

DOC SAVAGE stood on the bridge of the liner *Regis*. He had the big searchlight pointed in the air and was stabbing white light into the windy, dark heavens. He was sending S O S over and over again. It was not so much that he wanted help. He was endeavoring to show Ham, in the plane, where the liner lay.

"I sure hope somethin' ain't happened to Ham," said the apish Monk.

A stranger hearing the concern in Monk's tone would not have imagined that the hairy chemist had never, as far back as any one could remember, spoken a civil word to the dapper—and now missing—Ham.

There was a howl of powerful cylinders in the distance, and a plane came through the windy night, drawn by the blinking searchlight.

"May be a news reel or coast guard crate," said Monk, looking at the gloomy side.

It wasn't. It was Ham. He came in low, and his flying lights, red and green on the wing tips, began to blink out in code.

"Blazes!" Monk exploded, reading the signals.

Doc Savage's vague trilling came into being, but did not persist for long.

"Ham," Monk said, sourly, "has finally proved of some use."

Doc Savage went back to the staterooms and to the lounge, then to the bar. The bronze man's flake gold eyes were searching.

Ward, the steward, was in the bar, just taking a hooker of whisky.

"Here's to learning what that strange heat was," he toasted.

"Yes," Doc Savage said, and took his throat with both hands. "Here's to finding what the heat was."

Ward's convulsion threw the liquor in his own face. Sound tried to get up out of his chest and failed. He flapped his arms like a rooster, and did, finally, make a crowing noise of sorts. The stiffness went out of him.

Monk put his face close to Ward's, saw the man could understand what was spoken to him.

"Ham got them radio sendings you done," he gritted ungrammatically. "Ham was lost, the overdressed shyster! He just got back to the ship and blinked the news down to us with his riding lights."

"Ar-r-r-k!" said Ward.

Doc Savage released Ward's throat.

"Are Renny and Johnny aboard?" the bronze man asked.

The man Ward thought fast.

"Yes," he said.

Doc Savage looked at Monk.

"He's lying," the bronze man said. "Trying to hold us until the coast guard gets here, after which we are pretty sure to be arrested."

Monk grinned. There was nothing pleasant about the grin.

"Then we'd better get on our plane," he offered.

"Right," the bronze man agreed. "And we'll take this man Ward, if that is his name."

Ward paled. He gave a fluttering sigh.

"Might as well shoot me," he growled. "We'll drown trying to have that plane pick us up."

THEY did not drown. Doc Savage went below and started a pump forcing fuel out of a vent in the stern. This spread over the sea. It did not flatten the waves out, but it did stop them from breaking. It was the break of a wave that would do damage to the plane.

A few blinked signals with a light, then Ham came down. He leveled off, floated gingerly. The plane was like a big fly approaching a hot skillet.

"I bet Ham wishes he'd practiced up on his flying recentlike," snorted Monk, half anxiously.

Ham was a highly skilled airman. He proved it. He got down without even wetting the wing tip floats.

Doc Savage threw the man Ward overboard, then followed him. Monk came last. The water, covered with oil, was a messy place to swim in. But it was a pond alongside the breaking seas outside the oil area.

They climbed into the plane while it went up and down on the sea, twenty and more feet at a time.

Doc Savage took the controls, jazzed the throttles, then hauled them wide open. He set prop pitch and wing slots for the maximum climb. The ship wallowed down into a trough, up and up—and *up!* The sea fell away; the murk of the sky absorbed them.

"Whew!" Monk said. "Habeas, you just shook hands with the old guy with the scythe."

Habeas Corpus, the pig, grunted affectionately, ambled over and calmly bit the simian, Chemistry, by way of expressing satisfaction with Monk's return. Chemistry burst into an uproar which only a member of the monkey family could manage.

"Hey!" Ham howled, and kicked furiously at Habeas.

Habeas dodged with a precision gained of long practice. Chemistry picked up Ham's sword cane, which reposed on the seat, and brought it down with terrific force on Habeas. The pig's squeal put the monkey's earlier racket to shame.

"Hey!" Monk squawled, and threw the handiest thing, a binocular case, at Chemistry.

Ham made a snarling noise and started for Monk, gritting, "I'll skin you alive for that, you—you—orangutan!"

"Come on, you barrister fashion plate!" Monk invited.

Ward, the fake steward, plunged suddenly for the plane's door. He wrenched, got it open and set himself to lunge through into space.

Then he gave a loud gasp and lay down, partially out of the door, but not enough so that he fell.

Monk and Ham, their fracas forgotten, rushed forward.

Monk picked up the wrench which Doc Savage had seized from a cockpit pocket and thrown, knocking Ward senseless. Monk returned the wrench to the pocket.

"We should 'a' kept an eye on 'im," the homely chemist squeaked. "But I was so glad to see Ham that I was gonna beat his liver out."

Ham got Ward back inside, got the door shut.

"What are we gonna do with this client of ours?" he asked.

"Take him to New York and question him," Doc Savage said.

"It won't be easy to gouge out what he knows," Monk hazarded. "The guy was willin' to commit suicide a minute ago, to get himself out of our hands."

Ham asked, "What about Long Tom?"

"We will go over that south-southeast course from Montauk lightship and see what we find," Doc Savage said.

THEY did not find anything, except water and darkness. There was not even much wind, a fact which moved Monk to rumination.

"Queer thing about that wind," offered the homely chemist. "It was only blowing a gale over a narrow area around the liner *Regis*."

Doc Savage's regular metallic features did not change expression.

"The strange heat which wrought such havoc on the *Regis* was apparently confined to a narrow patch of the sea," he pointed out. "Heat causes expansion of the air. Cooling and resultant contraction of the air after the heat vanished would naturally cause a wind of some strength."

No more of consequence was said until they had flown the south-southeast course from Montauk lightship, starting far out to sea and working in until they plainly distinguished the winking of the light itself.

It was dark, so Doc Savage had not relied on the doubtful efficiency of their unaided eyes. He had used an infra-ray scanner—a contrivance consisting of two units, the first being a projector, literally a gigantic searchlight in power, which hurled invisible, fog-and-darkness penetrating light rays outside the visible spectrum. The second unit was a scanner, mechanical and electrical in nature, which rendered the infra-rays visible.

The complicated mechanical thing had shown nothing.

"Take the back course," Doc Savage directed. "We'll try it again."

He turned the controls over to Ham. The bronze man then removed the big film roll from an infra-ray camera which operated in conjunction with the scanner, and began going over the photographs of their back course with a magnifier. He saw, on one of the prints, something interesting.

It resembled a big swordfish fin, except that no swordfish fin would seem that large from such a height. On the edge of the print was automatically photographed the time to splits of seconds, and he calculated the position of the object from that. They flew back.

It was a wing of Long Tom's plane.

Doc Savage landed the seaplane near by, went overboard by the light of a flare, and swam to the wreckage. It was bad. A fragment of a wing, most of the air cells punctured. The lower end, where it had been attached to the plane, was badly mangled. Doc spent time there, examining.

He came back aboard with something in his bronze fingers.

"What's that?" Monk grunted. "A fish scale?"

Doc passed the object over for scrutiny. Monk, looking at it, revolving it in his hands, acquired a puzzled expression.

"Metal," he said. "Or is it? Seems kinda light. Looks as if it had been chipped off something."

Doc asked, "Did you ever see the broken glass from the container inside an ordinary vacuum bottle?"

"Eh?" Monk muttered. "This does look kinda similar. But blamed if I see the connection."

Doc did not elaborate.

They spent a long time hunting for Long Tom's body and did not find it.

Doc SAVAGE headed the plane toward New York City, flying very high up in the stratosphere. He kept the motor silencers cut in. He had reasons for the precautions.

The air had begun to seethe with radio reports. Listening to them plunged Doc Savage's party into a thoughtful silence. When Habeas and Chemistry staged a brief fight, neither Monk nor Ham interfered or insulted each other. They were deep in gloom.

Coast guard and news planes had reached the *Regis*. The radio operator had been found dead at his key. News that amazed the world was being flashed, and it could not help but make those in authority start wondering about Doc Savage.

The radio reports—the S O S—earlier had named Doc Savage as responsible for what was happening to the *Regis*. There was nothing to show the liner's operator had not done the sending, and the fellow was dead.

Dying testimony is invariably accepted by the public as the truth. Otherwise level-headed persons will regard as truth the mumbling of a dying man, although the victim may not have the slightest idea he is dying, and may well be trying to incriminate an enemy who is actually innocent.

"We're gonna have to answer a lot of questions," Monk muttered.

"Which will rather cramp our style," Ham agreed.

At almost thirty thousand feet, Doc Savage cut the motors and the plane drifted downward like a sighing ghost. The riding lights were extinguished.

Doc took binoculars and watched the Hudson River water front in the vicinity of the Hidalgo Trading Co., which was a combination warehouse, hangar and boathouse. The police, of course, knew that the bronze man maintained the place.

The warehouse was equipped with a remarkable set of alarms. A marauder did not have to break into the place to set off the system. Any one merely lurking near by would actuate capacity-balanced relays and give notice. The system was connected to a wire which caused an electric sign on a building some blocks distant to illuminate.

This sign was lighted now.

Doc Savage landed well up the Hudson, beached the seaplane, lashed it to a sapling, and headed for the downtown section of Manhattan with their prisoner.

The captive began to struggle, tried to shout. Monk, grinning fiercely, used a fist, and the man collapsed. They hailed a taxicab. It was dark where the cab stopped.

"Our buddy has passed out," Monk explained.

They kept their faces shaded riding downtown, and got out near the homely Monk's experimental chemical laboratory in the Wall Street sector.

MONK'S laboratory was something of a marvel of its kind. It was more complete even than the one which had been destroyed by the explosion at Doc's headquarters, as far as chemical equipment exclusively went. It was situated in a penthouse atop a financial skyscraper.

Monk's living quarters were adjacent to the laboratory. Monk went in for luxury and modernistic extremes. Everything was bright metal, glass or gaudy leather. Habeas Corpus, the pig, had a room of his own, equipped with a chemically purified and perfumed mud wallow.

Ham sneered nastily, as he always did, at the gaudy flash of Monk's place.

"The product of an animal mind," he sniffed.

Monk only grinned, and thought of times when he had made some choice and relieving remarks about Ham's overly dignified bachelor suite in a Park Avenue club so ritzy that even the bellboys were ex-dukes.

Doc went in to the laboratory. He had been there before, knew the distribution of chemicals. He began concocting mixtures.

"We'll need some electrical apparatus," he said. "Monk,

you rig it up. Ham, you keep the prisoner in another room, so he will not know what we are doing."

Ham hauled the captive away. The fellow had not yet regained consciousness.

Half an hour later, Doc Savage walked in and confronted the captive, now conscious. Doc carried a hypo needle. He calmly used it.

"What're you giving him?" Ham asked.

Doc Savage replied in Mayan, the ancient tongue, which he and his aides had learned long ago on a fantastic adventure into Central American jungles, and which they used to communicate with each other when not wishing to be understood by others present. Outside of themselves, there was probably not half a dozen men in the so-called civilized world who spoke the tongue.

"A drug which will loosen his self-control and make his mind more susceptible to outside suggestions," Doc Savage said, answering Ham's question. Doc spoke Mayan.

They waited. After a bit, the man began to squirm. He apparently had become scared. Doc glanced at Monk and Ham, and nodded.

"You've got to talk!" Doc Savage rapped, grimly.

The prisoner rolled his eyes. His lips shook back from his teeth in a snarl that had difficulty jelling.

"Hell with you!" he said.

Doc Savage produced a roll of adhesive tape, tore off short lengths and taped one of the man's eyes shut. Then Doc held a large, sharp knife in front of the fellow's other eye.

"When you change your mind, say so," directed the bronze man, and brought the knife down.

The fellow's eye closed involuntarily.

Doc worked fast. He flipped the knife aside, grabbed a chunk of ice which Monk had ready and worried the ice against the victim's eye. Ice passing over human flesh causes a sensation closely akin to a knife cutting.

Monk had an electrical contact ready. Doc slapped this against the man's eye. Tape already attached served to secure it to his face. Monk poured some warm water on the man's face.

The electrical contract delivered a steady, shocking pain that was realistic. The warm water felt like blood.

The man screamed. He floundered. They held him. He screeched so hard that spray flew through his teeth.

"This place is soundproof," Monk said.

"Which is lucky," Ham added, calmly.

Habeas, the pig, came in, grunting loudly, to investigate the screaming of the victim.

"Habeas," Monk said, "how would you like to eat this guy's eyes? O. K. Here!"

Monk then made lip-smacking sounds that were a very good imitation of a pig eating.

The man on the floor heaved. He acted as if he were about to have a fit.

"I think Habeas would like his ear," Monk said.

They used the ice, the warm water, and another electric shocking electrode to make the fellow think he had lost an ear. Had his mind been entirely rational, he might have known otherwise. But the drug had him dazed.

"I guess he ain't gonna talk," Monk said.

The prisoner only cursed.

"Like the ear, Habeas?" Monk asked. "Grunt if you did."

Making a visible signal, Monk caused his pet pig to grunt loudly.

"Swell," chuckled Monk. "We'll give you his other eye."

At that point, something about the proceedings struck Ham and made the whole thing look ridiculous, as indeed it was, except that it seemed to be working.

The man got rid of one last, long scream.

"Whatcha wanta know?" he asked, hoarsely.

"We wanta know where our pals are," Monk said.

"Who?"

"Long Tom," enumerated Monk.

"And Johnny and Renny," added Ham.

"What do I get for spilling?"

"I dunno," Monk said. "What you already got, maybe. Your eye, for instance. And your life!"

The prisoner writhed and swore.

"They said you guys never actually mutilated anybody!" he snarled. He made gurglings. "Oh, my—my eye!"

"Where's our pals?" Monk gritted.

"Uncle Penguin took them," said the man.

Chapter XI

THE POLAR GOAL

AFTER the man said, *Uncle Penguin,* every one was mystified enough to remain silent for a short interval.

"Huh!" snorted Monk. "This one-eyed, one-eared so-and-so is kidding us!"

"I'm not," said the captive.

"Gimme that knife," Monk commanded. "I'll cut out his other eye."

"Here's the knife," Ham said, helpfully.

The prisoner screamed once, horribly.

"Wait a minute!" he shrieked. "The *Uncle Penguin* is a boat! It's Cheaters Slagg's Polar exploration ship!"

Doc Savage said, "Is Cheaters Slagg the man who is known as Captain Montmorency Frederick Slagg, who charters his ship to famous explorers?"

"Check," said the prisoner.

"So he wasn't lying," Monk said in a disappointed voice. "Well, I'll just keep this knife handy in case he does."

Doc Savage took over the questioning.

"When did this thing start?" he asked.

"I ain't sure," said the man. "Five or six years ago, I think, when flying over the poles and exploring around them was so popular. Cheaters Slagg took an aviator and his plane down to the South Polar continent, and established bases for the fellow. It was while he was doing this that Cheaters Slagg found the valley."

The man took a deep breath, moaned, then went on.

"Two other people know of the existence of the valley,"

he said. "Or know where it is, that is. Derek Flammen, that explorer, is one. He was the aviator who had Cheaters Slagg's ship chartered five years ago when Slagg found the valley."

The man moaned more loudly.

"The other person who knows about the valley is that girl, Velma Crale," he wailed. "She found the place when she was flying around over Antarctica, exploring. She landed and found evidence that Cheaters Slagg had been there first. She came rushing back to the United States and hunted up Slagg and wanted to buy a partnership in the valley.

"She didn't have any money to buy it with. She wanted to buy it with her silence. She would keep still if Slagg would give her half. Slagg had a cheaper way of getting her to keep still. He decided to kill her. She was on that silver sloop, but she is a fox in skirts and she got away and started out to clean house. Only she didn't get so far."

Had the man not been under the influence of the drug, he would have realized that he would have fainted or at least become very weak from a wound so serious as that made by the removal of an eye.

"Where does Thurston H. Wardhouse come in?" Doc Savage asked.

"Damned if I know," said the man.

"What is in this South Pole valley?" Doc queried.

"I don't know."

"What caused that strange heat wave which struck the liner *Regis?*"

"I don't know."

Monk said, "Get me a whetstone, Ham, so I can sharpen this knife. I'm gonna have to cut his other eye out."

The prisoner reared up. He made loud garglings.

"I've told you all I know!" he yelled. "I was just a paid hand on the *Uncle Penguin!*"

He fell back on the floor, his head thumping very hard.

Doc examined him.

"Heart has stopped," he said.

HAM glared accusingly at Monk.

"You see," he snapped. "You scare normal people to

death, you missing link! Think of what I have to put up with!"

Monk was too sobered to think of a retort. It had not occurred to him that he would literally scare the prisoner to death.

"The guy musta had a bad heart!" he gulped.

Doc Savage was working swiftly. He went into the laboratory, got a long hypo needle of the type which Monk used to administer chemical mixture internally to experimental subjects, charged it with an adrenalin mixture, and came back. He administered it in the orthodox style.

The man began to breathe again.

It was not an unusual feat. More than one patient has literally died on an operating table, to be brought back by the use of magic adrenalin, which stimulates the heat into resuming its activity.

Doc made a telephone call. A few minutes later, an ambulance called for the man. It was a plain white ambulance, and the driver acted as if he knew Doc Savage. Monk seemed surprised.

"But the guy may know some more, Doc," Monk grunted. "He didn't tell us a thing about what this ship, *Uncle Penguin,* looks like."

"The man cannot talk for a good many hours," Doc Savage replied. "And he probably told us most of what he knew."

The ambulance left. Monk and Ham said nothing. They knew the ambulance would take the prisoner to Doc Savage's strange criminal-curing institution in upstate New York—a place where the patients were first operated on in such a manner that all memory of their past was wiped away, after which they underwent a course of training calculated to make them straightforward, honest citizens.

Not a soul, as far as was known, outside of Doc Savage and his aides, and those connected with operating the place, knew of its existence. Doc kept it quiet for the simple reason that such an unorthodox method of dealing with crooks would have called down a lot of criticism from well-meaning reformers with other ideas of how it should be done.

Doc SAVAGE set about the business of finding the ship *Uncle Penguin*. This took hours. They checked sailing records, and sent discreet inquiries to every ship in the near-by Atlantic Ocean which carried a wireless. They were hampered because they had to keep under cover.

At ten o'clock the following morning, a lighthouse attendant reported sighting the ship *Uncle Penguin* anchored in a little cove on the south shore of Connecticut.

Doc Savage, Monk and Ham, the pig and the strange-looking ape, all took a taxicab and went north to get the plane. But they did not get it, for the reason that police had discovered the craft where they had left it. Doc saw the guard posted, then directed their driver to head for Long Island.

The taxi driver had by now discovered who his passengers were. He said nothing about it, but passed a late newspaper back.

The headlines said police and government men were looking for Doc Savage and his aides. Warrants had been sworn for their arrest. The charge was suspicion of complicity in the affair of the *Regis*.

Doc, Monk and Ham got a plane on Long Island. It was a small amphibian, and Doc kept it in a farmer's barn for just such an emergency as this. The plane had folding wings, so it could be gotten in and out of the barn quite easily.

Doc flew toward the Connecticut shore.

THE south shore of Connecticut is rugged to a degree, and rather populated, but it has barren spots. This cove was one.

There was one ship at anchor in the cove. She looked as if she were a tramp, converted, and with bows re-enforced for breaking ice. Squat, beamy and ugly, she was riding deep in the water.

"That is probably the *Uncle Penguin*," Doc decided.

The bronze man produced a bottle of skin stain, and Monk and Ham hastily daubed themselves with it. They shoved paraffin in their cheeks, and began to look vastly different. Monk padded the top of his flying helmet with handkerchiefs, so that his head seemed much longer.

"You still look like an ape," Ham told him cheerfully, as he leered at Monk.

They tied Habeas Corpus and Chemistry back where they would not be seen. Doc got down out of sight, and Ham landed the plane. He taxied over the surface and sent a lusty yell toward the *Uncle Penguin*. He hailed in Italian, a language which he spoke with near native fluency.

"Where are we?" he asked in Italian.

Nobody on the *Uncle Penguin* seemed able to speak Italian, which was what Ham had hoped for. Monk joined the shouting, also in Italian. They created a perfect impression of a pair of noisy foreign aviators junketing and now lost.

Apparently, they decided to go aboard the ship in hopes of getting the information they desired. They broke out a collapsible boat with which the plane was equipped. This was opened in the cabin and the plane managed to get it through the door, at which point they had bad luck. Both Ham and the boat fell into the water. The boat upset.

Doc Savage was in the boat. The whole mêlée had been staged so that he could get from the plane into the water without being seen. The bronze man was naked, except for snug silk swim trunks and a belt containing numerous pockets for gadgets.

His teeth gripped the mouthpiece of a self-contained diving "lung" device.

Monk and Ham continued their troubles with the collapsible boat, Ham calling on all the ancestors of all the old Roman dieties to witness what he thought of collapsible boats in general. Monk contributed lusty yells in Italian.

The rail of the *Uncle Penguin* was lined with curious faces. The spectators were dressed as sailors. But there was something wrong. Their faces did not belong to men who believed in working for a living.

On the bridge, lounging with an exaggerated casualness that was plainly acting, was a burly man who wore spectacles with extremely thick, somewhat cloudy lenses.

"Cheaters Slagg!" Monk grunted at Ham, recognizing the man on the bridge from Doc Savage's descriptions.

"Shut up!" ordered Ham. "Abuse this boat, then get in and row toward the ship, and keep howling. We must hold their attention while Doc Savage gets aboard from the other side."

"Shut up yourself," growled Monk. "Don't tell me what to do."

Stricken with a bright idea, the two fell to abusing each other in the Latin tongue. At the same time, they rowed toward the *Uncle Penguin*.

At about the same time, Doc Savage eased to the surface on the other side of the vessel. He came up close to the hull, and he used his eyes and ears. Every one seemed to be at the other rail.

The bronze man stripped open the zipper mouth of one of the belt pockets and drew out a device which he always carried—a thin, stout silken cord with a collapsible grapple affixed to one end. The grapple was padded with sponge rubber. He tossed it upward with an accuracy born of much practice, and it hooked the rail.

He climbed, managing the by-no-means-easy ascent of the thin cord through the medium of tiny sliding clamps of a frictional nature. At the rail, he paused. It was a critical moment. But no one was in sight.

He went over the rail. A companionway gobbled him. The steps were steel, with rubber tread, and at the top was a tiny landing on which stood a bucket of suds and a mop which some one had deserted to go have a look at the plane and the two crazy foreigners.

Doc sloshed suds silently over the deck and made a few passes with the mop. This wiped out his wet footsteps.

It was dark deeper in the innards of the ship. Ventilation was bad, caused an oily smell. It was warm. Doc eased around an angle in the passage.

A hard, chilly point of metal that could only be a gun muzzle came against his side.

Velma Crale said, "I haven't been so scared since people rode in buggies, so be careful!"

Chapter XII

BAD LUCK HAD TWINS

DOC SAVAGE was disgusted for the next few moments. It had been years since an enemy had gotten close enough, unnoticed, to touch him with a gun muzzle. He had put in thousands of hours training his ears, his eyes, his sense of smell, to guard against that very thing happening.

The passage was full of oil odor. Somewhere, a generator was running. That had done it.

"You crop up in unexpected places," Doc Savage said.

The tip of the gun came away from his side slightly.

"Well, pluck my feathers!" Velma Crale murmured in astonishment. "I thought it was one of the crew."

Doc felt the gun touch his wrist. She was trying to hand the weapon to him.

"You want this?" she asked.

"No," he said.

"You'll need it."

He did not explain that he never carried a firearm for the reason that the possession of one, he believed, tended to make the carrier rely on the weapon, and to become correspondingly helpless when disarmed.

"How did you get aboard?" he asked. "And when?"

"Last night," she said. She whispered. "I hung on Derek Flammen's trail, and he came out here and I followed him. It was a dark night. I climbed up the anchor chain. Been looking around since."

"What'd you find?"

"Puh-lenty!"

"For instance?"

"Did you notice the water line?"

Doc said, "The boat is riding deep in the water."

"This tub is loaded to the hatches," said Velma Crale. "The freight is very funny. In the first place, the boat has been built over to accommodate some of it. There are long hatches on deck, and what seems to be huge lockers underneath them. I've done plenty of prying, but haven't been able to tell what is in the lockers."

"It was fortunate they have not discovered you."

"Sure. But it was easy. It's hot and stinks down here and they stay on deck. The hold is full of big boxes and crates. I opened one to see what was inside it."

"What was?"

The girl held back her answer a moment.

"A coil of rubber hose. The hose is reenforced to withstand great pressure."

Doc Savage asked, "Have you seen any of my aides?"

"Which ones?"

"Long Tom, Renny and Johnny."

"A pale runt, a long hank of bones, and a fellow with fists made for cracking walnuts?"

"That is them."

"They're aft."

"Show me," Doc requested.

"We'll probably get caught," Velma Crale complained. She led the way aft.

RENNY had been working on the bars in the door behind which he was confined. The bars were almost an inch thick and anchored to bolts, but Renny had bent them some. He probably knew he would never get them out, but working on them with his big fists helped vent out some of his temper.

"Holy cow!" he thumped softly when he saw Doc and the girl.

"Where are Johnny and Long Tom?" Doc asked.

"The first designated anthropogenetic specimen may be marked present," said Johnny's scholastic tone from behind Renny.

"Mark me down, too," said Long Tom.

"So all three of you are in there," Doc said, and gave the door some attention.

It was a steel door and stout.

The girl dropped a hand on Doc's arm. "Wait." She put

a question to Renny through the bars. "Where is Thurston H. Wardhouse?"

"Next door," said Renny. "I mean, next cell."

The girl tightened her grip. "Get him out first!"

Doc breathed, "Getting any of them out is going to be difficult."

There was some shouting from the deck of the ship. Ham was yelling in Italian from the water, demanding to know where he was.

Doc shoved a hand inside the cell.

Renny gulped, "Holy cow! What——" Then he went silent.

Doc went to the next cell. It had a barred opening in the door. The place smelled vaguely of cattle, and that odor tipped off the nature of the compartment. Explorers take milk cows with them nowadays. These prison cells had been the ship's stables.

"Wardhouse!" whispered Velma Crale.

Wardhouse put his strikingly handsome face against the bars where the passage light shone on it. The face was scratched, and the nose had swollen. One eye was black. The man wore no shirt.

There was movement behind him.

"Who's in there with you?" asked Velma Crale.

"Derek Flammen," Wardhouse replied. He had a voice which had been trained and sounded as if it belonged to a good radio announcer.

Derek Flammen, shoving to get close to the bars, asked, "Who's out there? How in the devil did you get aboard?"

Doc Reached for Velma Crale's mouth.

"It's Doc Savage," Velma Crale said before he could stop her words.

Derek Flammen emitted an ear-splitting yell.

"Help!" he squawled. "Doc Savage is aboard! Cheaters! Men! Help!"

Thurston H. Wardhouse set himself and drove a fist against Derek Flammen's ponylike face. Flammen fell down and began making aimless mumbling noises.

"He's the leader, Flammen is!" Wardhouse yelled excitedly. "I've suspected it! Now I know! He was in here pretending to be a prisoner, to pump me and see how much I had told Miss Crale!"

In a great rage, Wardhouse leaned down and slugged Derek Flammen again and again. Flammen stopped mumbling.

"Do not kill him!" warned Doc Savage.

Men came charging into the passage. They started shooting when they saw Doc.

THE passage was steel-lined. Indeed, the whole ship was steel. The bullets did a great deal of clanking and whistling. Doc shoved the girl, lunged after her. They sprawled into a convenient door.

"Derek Flammen!" Velma Crale gritted. "I hope he—hope he——"

Apparently she could not think just what she did hope. Doc crossed the cabin, which was on the port side of the ship. There was one porthole. He examined it. Portholes are made small to resist the force of the sea. A small boy could not have passed through this one.

"We won't be able to free the other prisoners!" Velma Crale howled.

"We had better concentrate on getting out of here," Doc told her.

The bronze man was working at the pockets attached to his belt. He got one open. The thing which he extracted was a small metal tube. He pressed a catch, and the end popped off. Came a hissing, an eye-hurting light.

A stream of molten substance came out of the tube, flowing like liquid. Doc moved the tube, pouring the stuff in a circle over the steel hull of the ship. The liquid, falling upon the steel, ate through it like hot lead through ice. An oval a yard across was cut out.

Doc kicked the center of it. The metal fell into the sea, leaving an opening through which their escape was easy.

He dropped the metal tube into the sea. It sank, and a cloud of steam and bubbles showed where it had gone down.

"Come on," he said.

The stuff he had used was a thermit compound, similar to the type employed in incendiary bombs during wartime. But now was hardly the time to explain that to the girl.

"Jump!" Doc directed.

The girl made no move to jump. Her face began to get queer, as if she were thinking wild thoughts.

"We can't make it," she gasped.

"We've got to try," Doc told her. "Jump."

Her face became more animated. She took her upper lip between her teeth. She still held her gun. She pointed it at Doc Savage.

"I hate to do this," she said, "but there's too much at stake. And you can maybe get away. Put your hands up."

Men were running nearer in the passage. Doc Savage said nothing.

"If I turn you over to them, they maybe won't do anything to me—won't kill me!" the girl gasped. "I'm going to try it."

Doc said. "You haven't many scruples, have you?"

"Depends on how you look at it. They won't kill you. They'll try, but you'll get away. You can't be killed."

Doc Savage stepped backward, went through the hole he had cut in the hull with the thermit. The girl did not shoot.

Chapter XIII

DEATH

VELMA CRALE tried to follow Doc Savage out of the ship. She was not quick enough. A gun crashed in the door. She shrank involuntarily from the noisy passage of a bullet close to her ear. Then hands had her.

"I am," barked Cheaters Slagg, "glad to see you! Hold her, somebody!"

Slagg dived on to the opening in the hull. The edges of this still smoked. He peered through, squinting. He got a fleeting glimpse of a bronze figure.

With wild haste, he emptied a revolver. The reports were so loud in the room that they left ears aching.

"Doc Savage!" howled Cheaters.

"D'ja get 'im?" asked some one.

"Hell! You know the answer to that!" Slagg waved his arms. "Two of you hold the girl! Four of you watch the other prisoners! Rest on deck!"

Cheaters Slagg charged above. He thought of something, whirled and bawled, "Let the boss out!"

"You mean Derek Flam——"

"Who'n hell'd you think! Get 'im on deck!"

Slagg ran to the rail, reloading his pistol. He lifted the weapon, aimed carefully at Ham—and Ham dived out of the collapsible boat.

"Snakes!" gritted Slagg. "He saw me!"

SLAGG then fired at Monk. He missed. Monk was tilting out of the collapsible boat. He made quite a splash and vanished.

"Get the machine gun!" howled Slagg. "They'll try to hide behind that boat!"

The machine gun was at hand. It was a heavy military weapon. Three men held it braced on the rail and a fourth wrestled with the firing lever and the job of aiming. The belt went through it so fast that it seemed to smoke, and a great shower of empty cartridges spilled along the deck.

The collapsible boat literally fell to pieces under the leaden storm.

Horse-faced Derek Flammen came charging on deck, knocking men aside. He took in the situation with a lashing glance.

"Get a rocket pistol!" he roared.

Rushing over, Flammen seized the firing controls of the machine gun. He pointed the weapon at the plane and it stuttered and hammered and the plane drifted a bit under the impetus given by hammering lead. The wings scabbed, the fuel tanks were opened, and a flood of gasoline drenched the craft.

"Here's the rocket gun," said a man.

Flammen took it, aimed. A ball of green fire came out of the muzzle, hit the plane, splattered, and the gasoline was set afire. Flames wrapped the plane like red tissue paper around a Christmas toy. Habeas Corpus and Chemistry popped out of the burning ship and swam.

Flammen was not satisfied.

"Start pumping fuel oil on the water!" he howled. "And put men aloft to watch that they don't come up!"

Men went aloft. The pumps started floating black, inflammable fuel oil through hull vents. That it might burn more readily, they mixed a bit of gasoline with it.

Flammen, leering, waved a bony hand.

"There's a sandy beach around this cove," he said. "They can't possibly get ashore without being seen and knocked down with our machine guns. And now I'll fix it so they can't come to the surface."

He tore a bit of canvas off a weather cover, applied a match to it, got it burning, leaned overside and dropped it into the oil which covered the water.

"Get under way!" he ordered. "Stand by in the mouth of the inlet!"

THE hull plates of the *Uncle Penguin* were thick enough, of course, that she was not bothered by the burning oil. She could not lie in the flames too long, however. The anchor came up, a man standing by with a hose and washing off the flaming oil as the chain passed over the wildcats. The propeller turned; the vessel swung lazily, and headed for the inlet mouth.

"Look sharp!" Flammen howled to the men on the masts with rapid-firers.

They looked sharp, but that was all the good it did them. Not a sign did they see of Doc Savage or his two aides.

They did see Habeas Corpus and Chemistry reach shore and scamper across the beach to safety. A man shot at Chemistry, at first thinking it was Monk, but missed.

The burning oil was spreading. It burned slowly, but spread swiftly. Black clouds of smoke arose.

"Lower boats!" yelled Flammen. "We can't let 'em get away under cover of that smoke!"

Lifeboats, motor-powered, were lowered, and armed men went ashore and took positions along the beach. The smoke went almost straight up, for there was not much wind. No one could possibly reach the shore without being observed by the armed watchers.

Fifteen minutes passed. No sign of Doc and his two aides was glimpsed.

Derek Flammen began to stare at the sky. It was very clear, the sun unusually bright.

"Rig the shields!" Flammen yelled.

Every one stood as if greatly shocked.

Cheaters Slagg began, "But——"

"Rig the shields!" Flammen snapped.

Slagg nodded, turned around and howled, "Stand by to rig the shields!"

Certain squads of men assembled along the deck. The manner of their assembly showed they had been trained as to what to do. Long, hardly noticeable hatches in the deck were lifted.

The vessel was equipped with an unusual number of short cargo booms and a good deal of loading tackle. These loading lines were attached to the contents of lockers under the deck hatches. Men hauled on the lines.

Folding sections of metal were dragged out of the lockers. The segments were designed so that they fitted over the metal framework of awning supports. Clamps held the parts in position.

The metal was peculiar, unusual. The outside was shiny, mirrorlike. The underside was dull, leaden. The sheets were, furthermore, quite thick. The men getting them in position labored and swore.

Only the parts of the vessel where men had to station themselves in order to operate the craft were covered.

CHEATERS SLAGG and Derek Flammen paced the decks, giving orders, cursing whenever the work of fitting the strange metal covering into position was bungled.

All of thirty minutes was required to get the peculiar awning settled.

Flammen looked at Slagg.

"All right," he said.

Slagg went below.

"Everybody under cover!" Flammen howled.

The men on shore came racing back to the lifeboats and rowed hurriedly to the vessel. The oil on the water had burned itself out now, and there had been no sign of Doc or his two companions.

The *Uncle Penguin* had changed its position to a marked degree. The awning of strange metal had given it an aspect vaguely like that of a shiny cigar. Viewed at close range, and in good light, the ship would have looked what it was—a vessel with a strange awning—but seen in bad light, or through a fog, it would have been baffling.

Long Tom, who had seen the craft under poor light conditions, had been baffled.

Amidships, atop the superstructure, men were opening hatches. It was an unusual spot for hatches. The men who had opened them scampered to cover.

The engines below decks were making a good deal of noise. A ship's motors are usually quiet.

It began to grow warmer. The heat increased rapidly. The march upward of the thermometer on the *Uncle Penguin's* bridge was almost visible. Men mopped perspiration.

Outside the little cove, a small ketch was sailing. No doubt those aboard were curious yachtsmen who had seen the smoke of the burning oil and noted the exotic appearance of the ship standing by the cove, and were sailing up to investigate.

The men on the little ketch began behaving queerly. They hastily rigged an awning. It did not seem to do much good. After a bit, the men on the little boat seemed to have some kind of fits, and then die. The ketch, no hand at the tiller, sailed into a reef, stove a plank and sank.

Aboard the *Uncle Penguin,* no man had ventured from the shelter of the strange awning which had been rigged. Almost every one was wearing thick, colored glasses, or had, if they were not working, dark bandages tied over their eyes.

The sun seemed to beat down with incredible force. Paint on the deck was blistering.

Derek Flammen watched the death of the men on the little ketch. He showed no signs of remorse.

"All right," he said into a speaking tube.

The heat began to grow less. Cheaters Slagg came up from below. The men rolled back the hatches on top of the superstructure.

Flammen grinned at Slagg. "That should take care of Doc Savage. If he's within four or five miles of this spot, he's done for."

Slagg nodded. "We're through with the bronze guy."

Flammen gave an order. Men fell to work taking in the strange awning and storing it in the deck lockers. The ship steamed out to sea.

A strong breeze was springing up—cool air rushing into the area.

CHEATERS SLAGG frowned. "Layin' in that cove was a mistake."

Horse-faced Derek Flammen frowned sharply. Derek Flammen's manner was vastly different now, from what it had been on the occasion of his contact with Doc Savage. He was cold, driving.

"It was necessary for you to pick me up," he said.

"You—and the girl," growled Slagg.

Derek Flammen looked intently at Slagg. His appearance underwent a change, becoming devillike. He seemed to sprout horns and a spike tail.

"Do I understand you are criticizing my methods?" he asked gently.

Cheaters Slagg looked at his chief—for it was now very clear that Flammen was the master. Slagg seemed to shrink a bit in height and his eyes grew wide and scared back of the thick, smoked glasses.

"Hell!" he gulped. "I didn't mean nothin'!"

Derek Flammen said, "Bring the prisoners to my cabin!"

Every man on board who could be spared from the task of making things shipshape for the open sea was ordered to get his gun and take a hand in escorting the captives. Special care was given Doc Savage's men.

The girl, Velma Crale, had been handled roughly. Her hair was askew, and there was skin missing from her knuckles.

Doc's three aides stood close together, saying nothing. They had made no move toward resistance.

Thurston H. Wardhouse stood apart, his erect, athletic figure defiant. He must have been forty, but he seemed to have the vigor of twenty.

Derek Flammen was drinking milk from a bottle and eating bread from a loaf. He tore off bread, chewed it, put his chin out to swallow, then scowled at the prisoners.

"Have the blacksmith cut four lengths of heavy chain,"

he ordered. "Handcuff pieces to this girl and Doc Savage's three men and dump them overside."

Cheaters Slagg asked, "You sure we won't need 'em?"

"I was keeping Savage's men to use against the bronze man, to decoy him some way," snapped Flammen. "I have decided that is too dangerous. The girl should have been shot the day she came to you and said she had found the Antarctic valley."

"We did our best in that direction," Slagg muttered.

Derek Flammen turned an angry horse face on Thurston H. Wardhouse. "Double-crosser!"

"I had no idea what you planned!" snapped Wardhouse. "My work was intended as a scientific boon to mankind, and not to be converted to their own use by such rogues as yourselves!"

"So we're rogues?" Flammen queried, sarcastically.

"You are! You have caused the death of scores of persons!"

"Do you realize, Wardhouse, that those people would never have died had you not double-crossed us?"

THURSTON H. WARDHOUSE showed his teeth unpleasantly.

"Miss Crale overheard you plotting to kill me so that you would not have to give me my share!" he snapped.

Flammen turned his horselike face on the young woman. "So you overheard that? I begin to see how you knew so much. Spied on us, eh?"

"All I could!" the girl said, defiantly. "I eavesdropped. That's how I learned you intended to grab me off the silver sloop. So I skipped out. I didn't dream you would cause the death of every one aboard."

"I hope you're not laying that on us?" Derek Flammen disclaimed piously.

"No," the girl jeered. "Nor that business of the *Regis*, either."

Flammen said, "Shoot her before you throw her overboard with a chain fastened to her ankle."

Thurston H. Wardhouse stepped forward. He seemed to care nothing for the menace of the guns all about him.

"Look here!" he rapped. "You cannot do a thing without me! You still need me."

"We might," said Flammen, "get along without you. I don't know. But as a last resort, we'll try it."

"All right!" gritted Wardhouse. "You'll have to try it if you kill these prisoners!"

Flammen scowled. He tore off bread, crammed it down, and poured milk after it.

"Let's get this straight," he requested.

"I won't do a thing for you if you kill these captives," said Wardhouse. "I won't have more killing. Keep them alive and I'll give you a hand. And believe me, you won't get along so easily without me. Or rather, my knowledge."

Derek Flammen eyed Cheaters Slagg. "What about it, Cheaters?"

"Shoot 'em," said Cheaters. "Hell with 'em!"

"So we'll keep them alive," Flammen growled. "Lock 'em up again."

The prisoners were dragged out. Passing a porthole, Long Tom got a glimpse of the receding U.S. coast.

"I got a notion to make a break!" the electrical wizard whispered.

"Don't be a sucker!" retorted big-fisted Renny.

"Eh?" Long Tom frowned at him. "First time I ever knew you to preach caution."

"I got me something you don't know about," Renny grunted.

"What?"

"A system, you might call it. Part of a system, anyway."

"When'll we try it?"

"When the time comes. Holy cow! Just keep your shirt on."

Chapter XIV

COLD LAND

FIVE weeks and three days passed. Long Tom, Renny and Johnny kept track of the days by making deep scratches in the thick layer of paint on the bulkhead. Their captors kept a guard steadily outside the door, and the light inside their cell was never turned off. They were not even allowed to talk. When caught talking, their next meal was denied them. It was either keep still or go hungry.

This did not bother them greatly, for all three were adept at talking on their fingers, and they did this. The discussion, long and involved, however, got them nowhere to speak of.

It was four o'clock in the afternoon—they had kept their watches and had them wound—when the engines of the *Uncle Penguin* stopped, and the anchor went down.

Renny knotted and unknotted his big fists. "Holy cow! We must be there!"

"Yeah," agreed Long Tom. "We're probably there."

Johnny, seeming more gaunt than usual, eyed them. "Unanticipated prognostications indicating precognition of our destination."

"It's a wonder," Long Tom grunted, "that those words don't choke you."

Johnny, using small words, said, "You guys talk like you knew where we were going. Do you?"

"Nope," said Long Tom.

They had discussed their possible destination for hours during the past weeks. They had obtained a general idea, or thought they had. For one thing, the ship had passed for days through a warm and at times unpleasantly hot climate.

They had decided this region was the tropics. Later, it had gotten cold. It was chilly now. Their captors had supplied them with sheepskin-lined coats and extra pairs of trousers.

They had seen or heard nothing of the other prisoners, Velma Crale and Thurston H. Wardhouse.

THEY sat there and listened. There were sounds of activity. Davits squeaking indicated a boat was being put over the side.

"Which means we're close to shore, I'm betting," Renny rumbled.

"An indefeasible opinion," agreed big-worded Johnny.

The three of them looked at each other. They had been conversing in whispers.

Suddenly, as if each were moved by the same thought, they all nodded.

"We'll try it now!" Renny breathed.

Renny got up. He put a hand in his pocket, brought it out, then went to the door.

"What in blazes is going on?" he asked, loudly.

The guard's face appeared on the other side of the bars.

"I thought you guys had your orders to pipe down and stay that way!" said the man.

Renny lifted his hand. There was a hiss, and a stream of liquid came out of the tiny water gun, cylinder-shaped, which his hand concealed. The guard gasped and fell on his face.

"Holy cow!" grinned Renny. "Doc's anaesthetic gas sure knocks 'em cold!"

The big-fisted engineer produced the second of two objects which Doc Savage had managed to slip to him during the course of the raid back in the tiny cove on the Connecticut shore. The first had been the water gun device. The second was another of the cylinders containing thermit compound which went through metal so readily.

Renny applied a bit of the thermit to the door lock. He squinted against the incredible white of the burning thermit substance. Then he hit the door with one big fist, above the section which was hot. The door came open.

"I hope we picked a good time," Renny rumbled, softly. "Come on, you two birds."

He went out. Johnny and Long Tom tramped his heels.

"Shall we free Wardhouse and the girl?" Renny growled.

"He's responsible for us being alive," said Long Tom. "I vote to do what we can for him."

"And the girl?"

"She's a snappy looker. I kind of like the idea of saving her."

They looked in the near-by ex-stable cells. Wardhouse and the girl were not there.

THEY mounted upward swiftly, anxious to get a glimpse of the spot where the ship was anchored. It had been cold below, but as they mounted, it became much colder. It was, they realized suddenly, probably some degrees below zero outside.

"*Ps-s-s-t!*" warned Renny, and stopped.

The others halted. They listened. Voices were coming out of a cabin to the right, and they crept near.

Cheaters Slagg was saying, "We've got enough stores here aboard to last about four months. Then we'll have to bring in fresh stuff. It will save time if we have a list of supplies shipped down and all ready and waiting at some South American port, say Buenos Aires, which is due north. Don't you think so?"

"I think so," said Derek Flammen. "Buenos Aires is due north."

"So I took the liberty of getting up the following lists of supplies that will be necessary in four months," said Slagg. "The lists are addressed to companies which handle this stuff, and the name signed is that of my own ship. My credit is good enough, so they will ship without any questions asked. Shall I radio the orders?"

"Are you sure it is stuff we will need?"

"Yep."

"Go ahead and send them, then. We've spent all of my money and all of yours on this project already. Or, at least, we've spent just about all. We've got to economize. But go ahead and send the radio orders for goods."

"Take 'em, Sparks," Cheaters Slagg said, apparently to his radio operator. "Get 'em off right away. And also get the news radio report and see if there is any report of this Doc Savage turning up."

"I copied the news a few minutes ago," said a non-descript voice. "There was a short item to the effect that no trace had been found of Doc Savage."

"Then we killed him and his two men in that bay," said Slagg.

To Renny, Long Tom and Johnny, listening, this conveyed their first inkling that Doc Savage was supposed to be dead. Horror held them for an interval, and only vaguely did they hear the radio operator make a remark.

"Doc Savage stands accused of the attack on the liner *Regis,* and on that silver sloop, and the killing of certain persons who died in the vicinity of that cove," said the radio man. "In fact, the world now believes Doc Savage caused that strange heat. They think it is some queer death ray which he invented."

"Hah, hah!" chuckled Slagg. "Well, send them radio orders."

The radio operator came out of the cabin a moment later. He was a man as nondescript as his voice. He walked with his head down, and the radiograms in his hand. There seemed to be almost a dozen of the messages.

He rounded the corner, walking forth boldly, giving no thought to anything but the messages in his hand, which he was to send.

He did not hear a slight hiss to one side. All he knew was that a strong attack of faintness suddenly came over him. He gritted his teeth. But the faintness was so great that he surrendered to it, lying down on the floor and going to sleep.

It was ten minutes later that the radio operator awakened. He consulted his watch immediately and learned this. He lay still for a few moments, collecting himself. His characterless face was worried. He held a hand over his heart, testing its beating. The thumps seemed strong enough.

The radio man got to his feet, observed the radio messages scattered about, and hastily gathered them up. He counted them. They were all there.

The operator went along the passage until he reached a door. He opened it and stood there, breathing deeply of the bitterly cold air. The cold air in his lungs made him cough. He sagged against the bulkhead, somewhat pale.

One of the crew chanced to walk up. The fellow stopped and stared. "Something wrong?"

The radio man grinned, hesitated, shook his head.

"Just had a kind of fainting spell," he muttered.

"You'll catch cold standin' there in the open door," said the other.

The radio man closed the door, and went on to his cubicle. It was warm there. A clock ticked, and a loudspeaker sizzled softly. The operator sat down in front of his key and began sending the radiogram orders.

The fifth one read:

HIDALGO TRADING COMPANY
NEW YORK CITY N Y
SHIP BUENOS AIRES ACE LATMAN INNER VALVE EXPANDER
STOP LATEST OVERTURN ON KNEE SLEEVE STOP BASE AD-
JUSTMENT DIVIDED STOP UNCLE PENGUIN SLAGG

The message sounded no more complicated than some of the others. So the operator went ahead with the transmission, and filed it along with the other sent messages.

When he was done, the operator got a stiff drink from a flask which he removed from a drawer. Then he stepped out on deck, drawing on a heavy fur coat, to get more fresh air. He seemed to be worried about the period of unconsciousness which he had mistaken for a fainting spell.

He walked toward the companion, and it was purely by chance that he happened to turn.

He saw big-fisted Renny creeping toward the radio room door.

"Yeo-o-o-w!" squawled the meek-looking operator. "Help!"

He got help, plenty of it. There was an avalanche of charging men. In a trifling time, Renny was set upon. Long Tom and Johnny were also flushed from places of concealment near by.

RENNY had many times proclaimed that he loved nothing more than he did a fight. In that case, the next five minutes must have been the happiest in his life. It was hardly likely he would ever go through a more short and violent fight.

The fray ended for Renny when some one bent an iron bar over his head, and he knew no more until he awakened when they tossed him onto a hard iron floor. He was naked, he learned. They must have stripped him to search him and make sure there were no more weapons concealed about his person.

A bit later, they tossed in clothing which was not his own, but evidently some from the ship lazaret. They were taking no chances.

Long Tom and big-worded Johnny were with Renny.

"I'll be superamalgamated!" Johnny groaned, feeling

numerous bruises, and examining his monocle, which had been, to his disgust, broken. From the amount of complaining he did about the monocle, which he never wore, a bystander would have thought him blind without it.

They made an examination of their prison. They decided it was the cell adjacent to the one from which they had escaped. It was this cubicle into which they had looked for the girl and Thurston H. Wardhouse.

Renny thumped a soft chuckle.

"You sound happy!" Long Tom said disgustedly.

"I am," Renny replied.

"An unpredictable eventuality," grunted Johnny.

"Yes," said Long Tom. "What're you happy about, for cryin' out loud?"

"I have been lucky," Renny said, cheerfully.

"Eh?"

"You see," Renny explained, "I hid that container of thermit in here before we got caught. Tossed it in when we looked in here for the girl and Wardhouse. Figured they'd put us back in here if they caught us."

"I'll be superamalgamated!" said bony Johnny.

There was a noise at the door. It opened. Two rifles menaced them.

Cheaters Slagg appeared, and stood scowling at them. He took off his colored glasses, polished them, and replaced them on his nose.

"Flammen and me had a talk," he said. "We changed our minds."

Something in his tone moved Renny to thump a query. "What d'you mean, you four-eyed tramp?"

Slagg showed his teeth at the insult.

"We've decided to make what you might call a permanent disposition in the case of you guys," he said.

Chapter XV

RADIO CLUE

ABOUT the time the emaciated William Harper Little-john was making his big-worded exclamation somewhere more or less in the vicinity of the South Pole, a messenger boy was walking a street in New York City. Modern radio communication is swift.

The message to the Hidalgo Trading Co. was about to be delivered. The messenger boy entered a ramshackle building on Thirty-fourth Street and mounted stairs to a musty door bearing the legend: "Hidalgo Trading Co." The messenger entered.

He was greeted by an elderly fellow in a green eyeshade and shirt sleeves, who signed for the radiogram. The elderly fellow put on his hat, took his umbrella, which he was never without, from the corner, and hooked it over his left arm, in such a position that he could reach, without too much trouble, the revolver holstered inside the umbrella, with his right hand. He left the premises and walked rapidly.

Fifteen minutes later, he was handing the radiogram to Doc Savage. The bronze man opened it, read.

He did not change expression, but his strange, exotic trilling sound came into being, persisted for a few moments, then ebbed away into nothingness. He walked toward a door.

The man who had brought the radiogram departed. He was an old fellow who did nothing but stay in the Hidalgo Trading Co. offices and perform a few simple jobs, of which this was a sample.

The messenger did not comment with any wonder on the fact that Doc Savage was alive. The bronze man did not habitually talk of what happened to him, so this minor cog in the vast enterprises which he maintained knew nothing of the episode at the bay on the Connecticut coast.

The affair of the bay had received considerable newspaper publicity, and Doc Savage had been connected with it—because of the weird heat, which was now attributed to some of the bronze man's scientific magic. No one had seen Doc or his aides near the bay.

No one, hence, knew that Doc, Monk and Ham had escaped the effects of the fantastic heat by remaining on the bottom of the bay, which was deep. They had been enabled to accomplish this through the medium of the tiny diving "lungs," self-contained, which they had carried.

They had not, as a matter of fact, remained under the bay at all, but had joined each other and worked out through the entrance to conduct a search—which had unfortunately failed—for the *Uncle Penguin,* intending to either sink her or board her.

They had spent the interval since in an intensive and world-wide, but thus far barren search for the *Uncle Penguin.*

Doc Savage, wanting the world—not so much the world as Cheaters Slagg, Derek Flammen and their mob—to think him dead, had not gone back to his headquarters atop the skyscraper, except clandestinely, to get such mechanism and apparatus as they thought might be needed.

This spot where they were waiting some trace of the bronze man's aides was a suite of rented rooms in a prominent and very busy hotel, from which they could come and go without too much danger of being discovered. Doc, however, had kept rather closely to the room, directing an intensive search for his aides and the ship *Uncle Penguin*—a search which had been barren of results. The *Uncle Penguin* had not been sighted in the last few weeks.

Doc reached for the doorknob of the adjacent room. He paused. Out of the room was coming an uproar. It had started explosively.

Ham was screaming, "You missing link! You awful mistake of nature! You hairy fright!"

"You lay off me!" Monk howled.

"Lay off you!" Ham screeched. "I'll lay you out on a marble slab! I'll trim your toenails off right next to your ears!"

Doc opened the door and went in. He was in time to see Monk go flying over a bed and around a table, Ham in close pursuit. Ham had his sword cane unsheathed and was slashing furiously.

"Now what?" Doc Savage asked.

"He's gone crazy!" Monk gulped.

"Crazy!" Ham screamed. "I'm just the camel that received the last straw!"

"I always knew you were something," Monk told him.

Ham squawled, "You know my pet, Chemistry?"

Doc Savage said nothing.

"Well," Ham gritted, "Monk, here, taught him to chew tobacco. And that's not all! That's not half of it!"

Monk got in the bathroom door, got the door ready to slam, and looked very innocent.

"I couldn't help it if the baboon likes to chew tobacco," he said.

Ham howled, "But you didn't need to teach him to spit in the pockets of anybody who happens to be handy!"

In his rage, Ham threw his sword cane. The homely Monk ducked wildly, and the long, sharp blade stuck into the wall behind him.

Monk reached for a chair.

"Let's postpone this a moment," Doc Savage suggested.

THE bronze man spread the radiogram open. Monk and Ham, each watching the other warily, drew close to read it. The text interested them particularly.

SHIP BUENOS AIRES ACE LATHMAN INNER VALVE EXPANDER STOP LATEST OVERTURN ON KNEE SLEEVE STOP BASE ADJUSTMENT DIVIDED STOP UNCLE PENGUIN SLAGG

"Blazes!" barked Monk. "The brass of the guy, ordering parts from us for his durn boat or something!"

"Look again, stupid," requested Ham. "That's a coded message."

Monk peered, reading the text once more.

"Blazes!" he repeated. "Sure it is. You take the first letter of each word, use your head a little, and you get——"

Doc Savage was already writing on the bottom of the radiogram what they got with that procedure:

S. BUENOS AIRES. ALIVE. LOOKS BAD.

"The letter 'S' probably means 'south,' " he said.

"Long Tom!" Monk howled.

"And Renny and Johnny!" Ham shouted. "They're alive!"

Doc Savage moved toward the telephone.

"We going down there?" Monk demanded.

"We are," said the bronze man, and picked up the instrument.

That Doc Savage had extensive interests other than the business of mixing in other persons' troubles and righting wrongs and punishing evildoers, not many persons knew. The true extent of the bronze man's holdings, no one but Doc himself knew.

They comprised transportation lines, air, water and land, industrial plants, and innumerable other enterprises. In none of these did Doc Savage actually appear as the owner, holding the controlling interest through dummies, the latter usually being actual persons in active charge of the interests themselves.

On the telephone, Doc Savage got in contact with the president, and as far as the world knew, the owner, of one of the largest Atlantic steamship concerns. A lengthy conversation ensued.

Doc's next call was to a concern manufacturing lighter-than-air craft. He spoke for some time, then hung up.

"Come on," he told Monk and Ham. "We are going to a little town on the New Jersey shore."

THE Hidalgo Trading Co. warehouse which was Doc Savage's airplane and dirigible and boat hangar was under police guard. The officials knew that the big structure, which did not look its part, was used by the bronze man. They had broken in and found the huge array of equipment.

It was hoped that Doc would appear. Everything was prepared to put the bronze man under arrest, should he put himself in evidence.

Late that afternoon, there was an unusual accident in the harbor. Two large ships belonging to the same transatlantic steamship concern all but met in a head-on collision in front of the Hidalgo Trading Co. warehouse. To avoid a smash, one ship sheered off—and rammed the warehouse, which was erected on a wharf.

There was a great uproar of yelling and whistling. The bows of the ship burst wide open, barrels of gasoline rolled out, and in some manner, caught fire. The ship swung and it looked as if ship and warehouse were menaced.

Men rushed in to save the contents of the warehouse.

Perhaps the largest object housed in the warehouse was Doc Savage's special stratosphere dirigible, a recent addition to his fleet of ultra-modern conveyances. This craft was particularly susceptible to damage by fire.

The roof of the hangar folded back in such a manner as to permit the departure of the dirigible. Before any one knew what was happening in the confusion, the little airship arose from the top of the warehouse hangar.

The police, at first, thanked their lucky stars that there seemed to have been some bystanders who understood the lighter-than-air ships. But when the dirigible droned away to the south, confusion seized the officers.

It was later found that the collision and fire had been mostly noise, confusion and smoke. The warehouse hangar and the ship had at no time been in any great danger. The police did some thinking, and questioned the officers of the two ships closely. That was all the good it did them.

Some one reported, just after sundown, seeing the dirigible dip for a time to the ground on the New Jersey coast.

No one reported a group of men, wearing greasy coveralls and talking the lingo of lighter-than-air fliers, who caught a train for the city, and later, another train for the plant where they were employed building dirigibles.

By that time, Doc Savage, Monk and Ham were aboard the dirigible, high in the stratosphere, and the automatic pilot had been set to take the craft directly toward Buenos Aires.

The police never were quite sure that they were the victims of an elaborate scheme whereby the bronze man had gotten hold of his airship.

A watch was ordered kept for the airship. But no one reported the craft.

THAT the dirigible should go unreported was not strange. Construction of the craft was the acme in lightness, and the lifting gas used in the ballonets was the result of a great deal of experimenting in the bronze man's laboratory; the gas had the lifting qualities of hydrogen and the non-inflammable merits of helium.

The ship was, furthermore, equipped with oversized rudders and elevators, vanes running the length of the craft, and at high speed, these exerted a marked lifting influence.

The conventional power plant consisted of Diesel engines and propellers, but there was also another method of high speed propulsion not so ordinary. A battery of rocket tubes were attached, and could, for short periods of time, give the craft a speed hardly equalled by the fastest of heavier-than-air craft.

The cabin was enclosed entirely within the all-metal hull, and was soundproof. It was insulated against heat, and air was supplied by oxygen apparatus when in the stratosphere.

Enough of the special Diesel fuel was carried for a nonstop flight to practically any point on the globe. Furthermore, the craft was equipped with a highly developed robot pilot—a contrivance which took over the handling of the ship completely and would guide the craft to any designated point on the globe. Those aboard could turn in and sleep throughout the voyage.

Danger of collision, the only peril existent in the stratosphere, and that a very remote one, was taken care of by sensitive alarms which indicated the presence of any foreign body in the line of flight.

The whole dirigible was a mechanical marvel. Its development and construction had cost more than the foreign debt of some European nations. Actually, it was still in the experimental stage.

Monk clambered up to the observation pimple on top of the bag after they had been under way for some hours and took a sextant shot of a celestial body. When he had figured his lines of position, he whistled.

"Brother, this baby sure eats space!" he murmured.

Ham snapped, "You might focus that great intellect on figuring out just what Derek Flammen and Cheaters Slagg have charged down to the South Pole after."

"A mysterious valley," Monk said promptly.

"Of course, pardon me! A valley. No valley anywhere else would do. They had to have a South Pole valley, and kill no telling how many people, stop ocean liners and kidnap mysterious Thurston H. Wardhouses off them, and no telling what else."

Monk sighed dramatically. "I might as well admit I don't know what makes this particular valley so attractive. And I will admit further that I don't know what that strange heat is."

Their quarrel continued, as it always did when they had nothing better to do. Doc Savage took no part in it.

The bronze man was up in the observation pimple with an array of delicate instruments, similar to those taken aloft by stratosphere balloonists. He made no explanation as to what he was doing. But after a time, he called down to Monk.

"Set the altitude governor a little higher," he directed.

Monk complied with the suggestion. Shortly, the dirigible was near its ceiling, surprisingly high in the stratosphere.

"Doc, what're you doin'?" Monk called.

The bronze man seemed not to hear, a small, and sometimes aggravating, habit which he had when questions were put to him which he did not wish to answer.

He employed repeatedly, in whatever experiments he was conducting, the bit of mirrorlike metal which he had found, weeks before, clinging to Long Tom's plane.

The plane, they knew now, must have been run down by the *Uncle Penguin,* so the bit of shiny stuff must be a flake off the peculiar metal shield which was fitted over the ship during the spells of fantastic heat.

THEY flew over Buenos Aires at night, so high that the city was a pale foam of lights on the infinite dark paunch of the earth.

South of Buenos Aires there would be no towns of consequence, so they checked everything, and finding all was well, set the robot due south. They had slept a good deal, which was well, for there was no more sleeping.

They flew very high, and searched incessantly for the ship *Uncle Penguin*. The searching was not done with the naked eye, or even with binoculars, but with a big aero-camera using infra light which penetrated fog and haze.

The pictures were developed and printed as rapidly as taken, and gone over with a microscope. They covered large areas and their fine-grain detail was breathtaking.

The *Uncle Penguin* had been indicated as being south of Buenos Aires. But directional terms are sometimes used loosely; an individual will speak of something being "north," when the direction is only generally that.

It was something similar in this case. They spent sixteen hours in as intensive a search as they had ever conducted in their lives. Hundreds of the wonderfully complete photographs were taken and scanned.

They reached the ice barrier at the edge of the Antarctic continent. In the enclosed, air-conditioned dirigible cabin, they did not notice much change in temperature, but it must be great. The ice barrier fringing the barren South Polar land was a vastness of scintillating, frigid upheaval.

They sighted the ship *Uncle Penguin* first on the photographed map of the barrier. They turned the dirigible back, and they used binoculars.

"There she is," Monk declared finally.

Chapter XVI

DERELICT

During some past warm season a field of ice consisting of some hundreds of acres of icebergs had broken from the edge of the frozen skirt of the South Polar continent, and the energy of the tides had kept this clear. The indentation was roughly a horsehoe, of considerable area. The water was free of ice, for the South Pole summer was beginning.

The *Uncle Penguin* lay at anchor in the bay. The dirigible sank toward the ship, and automatic controls took care of trim and elevators and rudders, it being merely necessary to seat an indicator level on the notched scale at the height at which it was desired to have the craft hang.

Doc and his aides used binoculars through the cabin windows, which were in two layers of nonshatter glass, with an insulating space between, after the fashion of the walls of a vacuum bottle. It was warm in the cabin.

The immobility of all time lay stagnant over the decks of the *Uncle Penguin* and the cold world below. No smoke climbed from the funnels or from the stack of the galley stove, which was aft and topped with one of those cylinder devices to keep out wind and rain called by sailors a Charlie Noble.

"It looks," Monk said, referring to the ship, "like a coffin, pointed at the ends."

"You're such a cheerful soul," Ham told him, "that somebody should knock your brains out."

Doc Savage disconnected the automatic pilot from the controls and took over the handling. He sank the dirigible to a point not more than a hundred yards above the ship, and brought it to a standstill. Their binoculars were powerful, and they used them carefully.

The lifeless aspect of the ship persisted.

"Blazes!" Monk grunted. "Where'd everybody go?"

They gave attention to the shore. It merely showed ice and snow. The snow looked as if it were a recent fall, rather heavy. Perhaps a yard deep on the level.

Doc touched the diving rudder control.

"We will land and search the ship," he said.

The dirigible eased downward.

"Somebody oughta stay aboard here," Monk said.

Doc advised, "You two draw lots."

"We'll match for it," Monk said, producing his trick coin with tails on both sides. He flipped.

"Heads," Ham said, as he inevitably did.

Monk grinned widely and said, "I hope you enjoy yourself."

The air was calm, and the sea as well, which was unusual for this harsh region. Landing the dirigible was a simple gesture. The craft was of a remarkably stout construction—had to be to withstand the strains of terrific speed.

The lower bulge served as a landing float. The craft came to a rest on the surface, as lightly as a feather, the propellers, situated well up on the bag, in the clear.

Ham took over the controls and maneuvered carefully. Had there been perceptible wind, he would not have been able to do what he did next—nurse the nose of the gas bag up against the side of the *Uncle Penguin.*

There was, of course, a tunnel inside the gas bag to the nose, where the mooring eye was situated. Doc Savage and Monk crawled to the nose, opened the hatch, and managed to drop to the deck.

Ham backed the dirigible away.

Monk was grinning over his deception with the trick coin. He swung along the deck with Doc. They entered the deck house, and wrenched to a stop. Monk's facial muscles collapsed out of their grin.

A man stood just inside the deck house. A gun was in his hand.

Monk saw the gun and acted instinctively. He lunged.

"Gimme that rod, bud!" he barked, and grabbed at the gun.

The man upset. He hit the floor with a noise such as a rock man might have made in falling. Monk stepped back, looking queer.

The man was frozen stony stiff, he realized now.

WIPING the hand with which he had touched the frozen man on his parka sleeve—both he and Doc wore regulation Arctic parkas now—Monk mumbled, "Why do such things always happen to me?"

Doc did not reply. He merely gestured slightly at the corpse. Monk knew that he was indicating the manner of the fellow's death. The man had been shot between the eyes.

"Well," Monk sighed deeply, "it ain't Renny, Long Tom or Johnny."

They went down to look for Renny, Long Tom and Johnny. Having found their cells earlier, they knew, of course, the location of the cubicles. But their three friends were not there. No trace of them could be found.

Monk stood in front of the cells and listened. His homely features became puzzled. "Say, looks as if this hooker were deserted!"

It was. They were not sure until half an hour later, when they had gone over the vessel thoroughly.

Nor was the fact that the vessel was unoccupied the only interesting discovery. The cargo holds were empty.

"Didn't the girl say there was a lot of boxes aboard?" Monk asked.

"She did," Doc agreed. "She mentioned particularly that one of the boxes held a large coil of rubber hose."

"It's gone."

Doc Savage returned to the superstructure and gave his attention to a huge hatch affair in the roof. This opened with an arrangement of pulleys and ropes attached to an electric motor, and opened to the sky a large room. This room was empty. But it plainly had held a good deal of machinery and apparatus which had been removed.

Doc studied the bases to which the mechanism had been attached. There were also electrical cables, obviously designed to carry a high voltage, which had been connected to the missing contrivances. Doc traced the cables into the hold.

They terminated in a compartment near the engine room, where there had been other machinery. A hole had been cut in a bulkhead to get this machinery to a hatch, so it must have been ponderous.

Monk's interest began to lag.

"I think I'll go have a look at the shore," he said.

"Go ahead," Doc told him. "There are boats hanging to the davits. You can probably lower one yourself."

Monk went out and lowered a small lifeboat, a feat that did not tax his gorilla muscular development. He noted that all other lifeboats seemed to be in place.

How, then, had the missing occupants of the *Uncle Penguin* departed? Monk emitted squeaky, puzzled grunts, as he pulled for shore. The mystery of the deserted ship was beginning to impress him as holding possibilities of becoming one of the major mysteries of the sea.

HAM was engaged in anchoring the dirigible. He had evolved an ingenious idea in connection with this. Using a bit of the thermit compound, he had melted a deep hole in the ice, and in this he had planted an anchor. The melted water was already freezing.

"Tell me how you're gonna get the anchor out?" Monk growled.

"More thermit, stupid," said Ham. "What did you find aboard?"

Monk told him.

Ham moistened his lips. "No sign of Renny, Long Tom or Johnny?"

"They'll be all right," Monk mumbled, voicing a hope rather than a known fact.

They finished the anchoring of the dirigible by dropping a stern anchor into the water which they found by sounding to be only three fathoms deep. Habeas Corpus and Chemistry were transferred to shore by dangling them by a rope from the end of the dirigible overhanging a flat cake of ice.

"Weren't you supposed to stick with the dirigible?" Monk asked Ham sarcastically, when the latter gave indications of taking part in a search of the shore line.

"I can keep an eye on it," Ham snapped.

They moved along the shore, scrambling over the ice with great difficulty. A little of that, and they went back to the dirigible to procure ice spikes which clamped to their moccasins, and helped keep them from slipping. The spikes augmented with a pair of long poles to poke out hidden crevasses, they crept along the edge of the ice barrier.

While the sea could be classified as perfectly calm, there was a swell, and this rushed in and out of ice cracks occasionally with loud, eerie sobbings. This uncanny noise bore somewhat on their nerves.

Habeas Corpus, the pig, did a great deal of bounding about to counteract the effects of the cold. Chemistry, the monkey, stuck close to Ham. Chemistry was equipped with a coverall garment of sheepskin which lent him a remarkably human appearance. Chemistry for once did not squeak and try to take his clothes off, a habit which Ham had tried to break.

Monk, to counteract the somewhat spooky feeling of the chilly, tumbled masses of ice and snow, was elaborating on what they had found aboard the *Uncle Penguin*. He was telling about the frozen man, how he had seized him.

"My hair ain't come down off end yet," he grumbled. "It was gloomy in there, kinda, and I couldn't see but what——"

An entirely new voice addressed them, coming from the snow perhaps twenty feet ahead.

"I hope it's light enough for you to see a live guy with a gun," the voice said.

Chapter XVII

GUERILLA SCRAP

Monk lived up to his apish appearance in that his reactions frequently had a bit of the animal in them.

Startle an animal and the instinctive reaction is almost invariably sudden movement. Monk moved suddenly now.

He flopped to one side, the idea being to conceal himself in the snow. He succeeded beyond his expectations. There was a crusty sound of breaking snow, and Monk vanished completely.

"Yeo-o-o-w!" he howled.

He always howled when something violent was happening to him, or he was doing something violent. The sound seemed to sink away into the depths of the earth.

Ham stood petrified. Forgotten was the surprise of the voice which had hailed them with such brittle unexpectedness from the snow. Tragedy was like an animal on Ham's face. He thought a world of homely Monk, with whom he always fought. It showed on his features.

The man who had remarked that he hoped it was light enough for them to see a live man with a gun got up out of the snow where he had been lying, covered over completely except for an eyehole. He swung a dark revolver at his side. His face was aghast.

"Holy cow!" he rumbled. "I wouldn't have had anything like that happen for the world!"

Ham yelled blindly, "Damn practical jokes! If Monk's dead, this caused it!"

Then Ham worked toward the crevasse. He did so gingerly, exercising extreme care. The crack was of considerable scale, they could see now.

Renny worked closer also. "Have you seen anything of the girl?"

"No," Ham growled.

"Or four guys with rifles?"

"No." Ham used his shoe spike to dig a little pit in the ice.

"That girl is a pain," said Renny. "She makes me ache all over."

Ham hooked his toe in the little pit and lay down to hang his head into the ice crack. He did not say anything.

Renny crept forward. "The crowd left the ship and went inland. They left five guys with rifles to guard me and the girl. I got us loose. There was a fight, and one of the four guys was shot by the others by mistake. Me and the girl got ashore.

"Me, that's the last I saw of the girl. She gimme the slip. I've been looking for her, and the three guys with rifles have been looking for both of us. As far as I know, nobody has seen anything of anybody else."

Ham said nothing. He peered into the ice crack, clinging precariously. He could see nothing, because of the gloom. Something suspiciously like a sob came pumping up out of his chest.

"I'm sorry," Renny rumbled contritely.

Renny leaned forward himself to see. There was a hissing, and snow slipped into the crack.

"Holy cow!" Renny boomed as he shot into the depths.

The snow made rather a rumble falling into the crack, and it was not a pleasant sound. Ham drew back, shaking so that he was afraid his toe would slip out of the pit he had dug. Habeas Corpus and Chemistry came up behind him and began to squeal and chatter.

It was some minutes before Ham got himself composed. His chest was convulsing a little. Tears were toppling from the corners of his eyes. He sobbed once. He was thinking of Monk.

He leaned over the ice crack. A snowball hit him in the face.

"Big blubberbaby," Monk said, cheerfully.

NOTHING escaped Ham for perhaps ten seconds. "You both all right?"

"This thing is only about a dozen feet deep," Monk chuckled. "There's soft snow on the bottom. I didn't say anything after I fell in because I was getting even with Renny."

Ham got up and stepped back. He looked around. There was a slope behind him, three or four feet deep in snow. He climbed the slope, slipping a good deal.

"This is getting even with you two practical jokers," he called, and threw his weight against the snow. It slid. He managed to keep from following it because of the spikes on his shoes.

The snow poured into the crack to a depth of several feet, and the wrathful comments of Monk and Renny came up through it. They were both streaming perspiration when they managed to get on top, work down the crack a short distance, and scale the sides.

Digging snow out of his garments, Renny rumbled, "This is a hell of a time for horseplay!"

"Where's Johnny and Long Tom?" Monk asked.

"Cheaters Slagg, Derek Flammen and their crowd took them along.

"Where to?"

"The valley."

"Where's that?"

"Don't ask me," Renny thumped. "They had planes in the hold of that boat, believe it or not. Seaplanes. Three of them. They assembled the darn things. There was a lot of freight in some boxes in the hold, too. They took that stuff out, and the planes took it away. It was quite a cargo. They made darn near fifty plane loads, altogether, I guess."

Monk paused dramatically before he put his next question.

"What's behind all of this business?"

"I still," said Renny, "don't know."

"Does that girl know?"

"I think so," replied Renny. "I asked her what was behind it. I think it is something in the valley they're after. I asked her. She just laughed in my face, and said she was not going to tell anything as long as there was a chance of her getting hold of the thing herself."

Renny's voice when he mentioned the young woman was pained.

"You don't seem to like her," Monk chuckled.

Renny pulled his parka hood away from the side of his face to exhibit a scratch of no small proportions.

"Look," he said. "And I just told her I thought she was as big a crook as the others."

"I'm beginning to like that gal," Monk said, "in spite of her being greedy."

"Some day a nice miracle will happen," Ham said.

"Huh?" Monk frowned.

"Something in skirts will come along that you won't like," Ham told him.

Renny suddenly stiffened.

"Holy cow!" he thumped. "There's somebody——"

He was too late. A man eased around a near-by hummock of ice, the stock of a submachine gun cradled against his shoulder.

HE was a man with a lean face, and probably a lean body also, but the voluminous subzero clothing which he wore lent him a more plump aspect. The submachine gun was fitted with a trigger in a guard so small that a finger encased in a glove could not have been thrust inside the guard.

The man had evolved a patent of his own. He had lashed a thong to the trigger and was holding the other end. He could wear his gloves and still shoot. All he had to do was pull the thong.

"Is this your man with the rifle?" Monk asked thinly. "Or one of them, at least."

"It's one of them," Renny rumbled gently. "Only he had a rifle the last time I saw him."

The man said, "You guys better get your hands high. And what I mean, *high!* If you're carrying any little pistols inside your gloves, better not try to use them."

Monk was not carrying anything but his fingers inside his gloves, but he checked the pistol idea in his memory for future use—if he was to have any future. They held their hands high. This man was not the kind who would stand any foolishness. Not with a face such as he had.

The man with the rapid-firer crunched a bit closer through the snow.

"Where's the hobgobliness?" he asked.

"The girl?" Renny shook his head carefully. "You've got me."

"I hope to tell you I have. You left the boat with the girl, didn't you?"

Renny nodded.

"What became of her?"

Renny scowled. "She caught me at the top of an ice ridge, gave me a shove, and that's the last I seen of her. It was snowing, so I didn't get to trail her far."

The man with the submachine gun sighed. "She's certainly a brisk creature."

"She certainly is."

"You don't know where she is?"

"No."

"You don't know where Doc Savage is?"

"No," said Renny, truthfully.

"Then you're of no use to me," said the man.

He pulled on the thong attached to the machine gun trigger.

Chapter XVIII

MAROONED

THE machine gun emitted lead and flame and noise. It behaved strangely, jumping away from the man's shoulders as he let go of it, stopping firing as the thong slackened, then starting again as the thong tightened. The end of the thong, it seemed, was looped about the man's glove, which caused the weapon to hang and roar at random after he had dropped it.

The man had been hit in the head with a lump of ice. He was knocked out, but still on his feet, swaying, tilting first one way then another, some instinct of balance keeping him erect.

Snow geysered all about as the machine gun swiveled and roared. Monk ran toward the spouting weapon, intending to grab it, but the stream of lead hosed toward his feet, and the homely chemist changed his mind and retreated with ungainly leaps. Then the man fell over in the snow, the thong slackened and the gun went silent.

Doc Savage appeared from behind the ice pinnacle, where he had stood when he threw the ice lump. He made no perceptible sound as he moved forward.

"Whew!" gulped Monk, "How long were you there, Doc?"

"Quite a while," the bronze man said.

Monk wiped cold sweat. "I'd hate to think you arrived right at the last minute, because I'd keep thinking what if you had been a minute later."

THE bronze man went to the machine gunner, picked up the gun and tossed it to Ham, who caught it and absently began to warm his hands on the hot barrel while he studied the face of their late captor. Renny came over and also eyed the fellow.

Doc examined the fellow, found him breathing. "He should be able to tell us quite a few things."

"I should hope so!" Renny boomed. "I'm getting tired of not knowing what this is all about."

Doc Savage seemed about to say something more, but instead, spun and began to race across the snow. Monk and the others, not knowing what was wrong, but realizing it must be something drastic, plunged after him. They slipped and floundered, their best efforts making no more than half the speed of the bronze man.

A moment later, they knew what Doc had heard. It reached their ears, the clanking of metal from the spot where Ham had left the dirigible anchored. They came in sight of the aircraft, and the worst of any fears they might have had were realized.

Velma Crale was in the airship. The noise they had heard was her efforts to free the anchor cable. She already had the stern line clear, was working on the bow line. She got it off.

The dirigible drifted away. The remarkable young woman, standing erect in the nose cockpit where she had been working to free the anchor line, made a derisive gesture at them.

HAM'S not unhandsome face was a blank study as he watched the dirigible slide away from shore. The craft had been left in his charge, and there was no sensible reason why he should have left it and accompanied Monk, except that that course promised, at least, exercise.

The airship did not rise from the water, for the reason that the buoyancy had been decreased for the landing, and some ballast would have to be dropped. While there was hardly enough breeze to ripple the water, there was, it became apparent, some air movement, for the gas bag was carried away from the ice barrier at a surprising speed.

Doc Savage began shedding outer garments as he ran. It became apparent that he intended to plunge into the icy water and attempt to overhaul the dirigible, which was now some distance out from the ice barrier. Indeed, he evidently considered more speed possible in the water than across the slippery ice and treacherous snow, because he veered over abruptly and dived.

Chill water boiled up, frigid and blue, where he disappeared. He came up almost at once and began to swim with a terrific overhand stroke which made him seem to all but travel on top of the water.

Then the dirigible's engines started.

The young woman must have fathomed the starting controls, which were not difficult, especially to one who was a world-famous aviatrix, as was Velma Crale. The gas bag scudded across the surface, got out of the bay, and began to heave up and down on the deep sea swell. But it kept going.

Doc Savage turned back.

The dirigible kept on the water for some time, evidently while Velma Crale puzzled over the handling of the craft. Then it arose abruptly from the surface, and went up with rather unnatural speed.

"She dumped too much ballast," Renny rumbled. "First thing she knows, she'll be up so high the gas bags will break or something."

"She got it going, at least," Monk pointed out. "And that's something, what I mean."

"There's no accounting for tastes!" Renny snorted.

"Eh?"

"You like her. O. K. O. K. I only hope you have a run in with her and she knocks hell out of you."

Doc Savage was donning the clothes which he had removed, having first stripped off his wet garments and wiped himself comparatively dry. He seemed impervious to the intense cold.

"We'd better get back to that prisoner," he said.

Nothing in his tone or expression showed that he felt any pique over the loss of the dirigible.

Ham said nothing as they trudged through the snow, and crawled, with infinite difficulty in some cases, over the ice hummocks. But the dapper lawyer was not wearing a happy countenance.

"That was my fault," he groaned.

"Sure it was," Monk said, cheerfully. "You're more bother than you're worth."

Seeing Ham miserable always made Monk inordinately cheerful.

They rounded a mound of ice and saw that the man who had held the machine gun was gone.

THE means of the man's departure was speedily evident. The evidence was there in the snow. Tracks. Two men. They had carried him away.

"His two buddies!" Renny rumbled. "Holy cow! They must have spotted him."

Doc Savage said nothing. He was already running along the trail. It led directly toward the bay.

Renny had a premonition. "They've reached the water, and I think they've got a folding boat stashed there somewhere. It can't be a regular boat, because I hunted for it. Must be a folding boat that they can hide."

It was. And they had it unfolded and were well out in the little bay, rowing madly. Two men at the oars, the third still senseless.

"I'll put a stop to this!" Ham barked, and lifted his machine gun, the one they had taken from the would-be killer.

"Stop!" he yelled warningly. "Heave to!"

Five bullets from a revolver came racketing back by way of an answer.

"All right!" growled Ham. "They asked for it! I'll sink that canvas boat so quick they won't know it."

His machine gun banged five times and stopped. He glared, yanked the magazine off and looked at it.

"Empty!"

The three men got on the *Uncle Penguin*. The craft was equipped with Diesel motors, which could be started without any preliminary delay of getting steam up. The anchor donkey engine made a great deal of noise pulling up the anchor. The ship got under way and stood out to sea.

Doc Savage stood on the edge of the ice barrier and watched the *Uncle Penguin* go. His metallic features registered none of his feelings.

His three aides, a short distance away, were more vocal.

"This is what is technically known as a pickle," Renny offered gloomily. "Marooned."

"No transportation," added Ham.

"No food," contributed Monk.

"And a thousand miles from nowhere," groaned Renny.

"Conservatively that."

Doc Savage had taken his attention from the *Uncle Penguin,* and was staring upward. The dirigible was very high, but seemed to have ceased rising. Evidently Velma Crale had discovered how to manage the buoyancy.

After a time, the airship began to move. The girl had learned to fly it, thanks to her skill as an aviator.

Doc Savage worked his way to the top of the highest ice hummock in the neighborhood. From his clothing he took what resembled a pair of goggles—goggles with lenses as thick as condensed milk cans, and absolutely opaque.

MONK and the others stared. They knew what the goggles were. They made visible to the eye certain wave lengths of light ordinarily invisible. Doc Savage used them in conjunction with an infra-light searchlight on occasion.

They looked on, their breath running past their lips, as long plumes of steam. They were puzzled. Doc, they knew, had no infra-ray searchlight with him. Anyway, what good would it do?

Doc looked up at the dirigible, through the infra-light goggles. He seemed satisfied.

"Want to try it?" he asked, and handed the goggles to Ham.

Ham took them, donned them. "Jove!"

"What is it, shyster?" Monk asked.

"That dirigible shows up like a lighthouse," Ham said.

Doc Savage said. "You all know that there is an infra-ray searchlamp mounted on the underside of the dirigible for scouting at night."

Renny rumbled, after taking the goggles from Ham and clamping them to his own eyes, "Holy cow! We can follow that dirigible's course for a hundred miles or so!"

"Depending on whether it flies high enough," Doc Savage corrected.

Monk said, "You turned that infra-ray searchlight on before we left the dirigible anchored, huh, Doc?"

"As a precaution," the bronze man admitted.

"And we're gonna set our course by the way it's flying?"

"Exactly."

Chapter XIX

COLD TRAIL

CONTRASTING with the North Pole, which is an expanse of sea overmassed with ice, the South Polar area is largely continent. But it does not follow that the South Polar region is more kind to human existence, or the existence of any other thing for that matter. It is probably true that there is no desert on the face of the earth that does not support more life than a corresponding area of the Antarctic continent.

Monk was all for starting immediately after they had determined that the dirigible was flying almost due south. Renny and Ham saw no reason why this was not a good idea.

Doc Savage, however, delayed nearly twenty-four hours and went fishing. He had, it developed, a few fishhooks in his clothing, and the silk cord attached to his very useful grapple hook served as a line. They caught three fish. They were evil-looking fish, oily to the taste, but one had the quality of size. Doc dressed the fish, let it freeze, made it into packs, and they set out.

That was the initiation of one of the most strenuous periods of their lives. They had penetrated unmapped jungles in a number of far corners of the earth, and they had been in the Sahara, Death Valley, and that most unknown of all deserts, the Rub-El-Khali of Arabia.

But, as Monk expressed it, "Say, we wasn't up against nothin', before this."

IT had not been uncomfortably cold along the coast,

due no doubt to the proximity of the water, but once they were inland, across a range of low, rugged and indescribably bleak mountains, the chill became something to talk about. Not that they were in danger of freezing to death.

"But I'll bet it'll freeze doorknobs down here in the winter," Renny declared.

The way became, to the eye, perfectly level. But that smoothness was deceptive. Snow and ice overlaid the terrain, and huge cracks were frequent.

"It wouldn't be so bad, if it wasn't for this snow," Ham grumbled.

The snow was about three feet deep on the level, and being a recent fall, was soft, fluffy. They had no snowshoes, but they would have done no good in snow like that, anyway.

They saw absolutely no living creature during the first four days. On the fifth day they got three penguins. They ate them at once.

"I know now what the world's worst meat is!" Monk complained.

Habeas Corpus and Chemistry managed, with a bit of aid from their owners, to fare moderately well.

"That dang Chemistry's hide will make good thongs for snowshoes, if we find something to make the frames out of," Monk declared.

"And the hog will make bacon," Ham countered. "Although I can't say I look forward to the prospects. That hog would take a lot of cooking at the best, and we haven't anything to cook with."

On the sixth day, the wind began to blow.

IT came up quite suddenly, that wind. They forged ahead, without giving it particular attention, at first; but before long it was all but upsetting them at times. And it was doing terrible things to the snow, scooping the loose flakes up and hurling them along in a stifling, stinging mass.

They had to hole in. Travel was impossible. Breathing in the gale was difficult. So they worked into a drift on the lee side of a boulder, made scarred and strange by ages of Polar elements, and huddled close together for warmth.

Their parkas, with the exception of Renny's, which had

been supplied him by the *Uncle Penguin* crowd, were equipped with chemical warmers which were efficient, but they intended to use them only as a last resort, for the reason that the chemical supply would last only a limited time.

They were holed up for so long that Monk and the other two lost track of the day, and it was only the fact that Doc Savage's watch had a calendar hand that convinced them of the day.

The wind did not die. They decided to go on, anyway. It was really Doc Savage's conclusion. He did not explain how he had reached it.

Torture marked their every step now. Their moccasins wore through, and they had to sacrifice other garments to wrap their feet. The supply of fish, which had seemed heavy at first, became unpleasantly light.

The wind did not blow so strongly now. But there was still more than a hatful. The temperature, strangely enough, did not behave in a normal fashion. It became, if anything, a bit warmer. The wind did not carry as much snow now. It cleared.

And they found their dirigible.

Found what was left of it, rather. Which was not much. The framework, and that was scattered. The hull covering, thin and superlatively stout and light metal alloy. The fragments were mangled and scorched.

"A bomb," Monk said.

Doc Savage looked over the ruin without comment. He had spent the ransom of kings on the superlative craft, and now it was lost. If the financial blow irked him, he did not show it.

"The girl!" Monk gulped, hoarsely.

They dug through the snow. They lifted the mangled skin sheets of the dirigible, moved the elaborate, superlight girders. They combed an area of many acres, but they did not find the girl.

Doc pointed out deductions which were the result of certain observations.

"There is a hole blown in the ground, so the craft was destroyed after it landed, or was forced to land," he said. "Our search has turned up no trace of the numerous boxes of equipment which we had aboard. The dirigible was, therefore, rifled before it was blown up."

Monk heaved a vast sigh of relief.

"Maybe the girl was taken away, a prisoner," he suggested.

Doc Savage did not comment, for he was examining a metal case which he had found intact, and which held what at first glance had the appearance of pills of some kind. The searchers of the dirigible, before its destruction, must have thought them pills. Actually, they were concentrated food tablets.

The supply would keep the four of them alive for weeks.

"You fellows will be all right here for a time," Doc said.

"Holy cow!" Renny rumbled. "Where are you going?"

"On a bit of a scouting trip," Doc replied.

THE bronze man's scouting trip was not as protracted as he had expected. His first move was to search for signs of planes having landed in the neighborhood. They had. More than one of them; three, it appeared. And three fitted the situation, being the number possessed by the enemy.

The landings, as well as the blasting destruction of the dirigible, had taken place prior to the wind. But a few traces remained. There were, moreover, tracks, these proving conclusively that all of the raiding party had not been in the planes. Doc searched. He found a trail, made by men, heading a bit west of south.

"This alters things," the bronze man told his aides. "It means the mob has headquartered somewhere not far distant. Probably beyond that high ground. We will push ahead together."

The high ground mentioned was difficult, at first, to see. The utter flatness of the Antarctic waste made the terrain seem saucerlike. But, after a bit of comparative surveying, Monk, Ham and Renny did perceive that there was a range of hills to the south.

The trail they followed—which Doc Savage followed, rather, for only once did his aides see a sign of it—led toward the hills. Nearly twelve hours elapsed, however, before they were climbing the ridge.

They had noticed one thing. It was a great deal warmer here. Very little snow remained on the rocky earth. Pools of melted snow water stood everywhere.

At Doc's suggestion, they used more caution. The bronze man remarked simply that they could never tell what they might find, and care was no great strain.

Thus it was that they crept furtively up an eminence of stone, peered over and were confronted with a sight that was not only unexpected, but incongruous.

"Blazes!" Monk gasped. "A guy walking around the South Pole carrying an umbrella!"

Chapter XX

PRECIOUS VALLEY

THE man was one of the *Uncle Penguin* crowd; they had all seen him aboard the ship during the excitement in the Connecticut shore cove. He was a lean fellow with big bones and a rosy sunburn.

The really startling thing about the man, however, was the parasol which he carried. It was no ordinary umbrella, except in shape. In size, it approximated the big parasols used by beach loungers. It came down farther at the edges.

In fact, it resembled a big toadstool on a very thin stem. It was made of a shiny metal, apparently the same stuff that composed the strange plates which had shielded the *Uncle Penguin*.

The man was carrying it carelessly, making no particular effort to stay under it. Under his left arm was tucked a rifle fitted with a telescope sight.

Climbing to a prominent point of rock, the man searched out a crack, stuck the handle of his strange umbrella into it, and proceeded to build himself a seat out of stray boulders.

He consulted his watch, then glanced upward several times. He seemed in no hurry.

Unexpectedly—at least to Doc and his men—a weird, undulating sound came vibrating across the Arctic wastes. It was a sound familiar in civilization's population centers, but one of the last noises to be expected here.

"Police siren!" Monk gulped.

"Some kind of a signal, obviously," Ham corrected.

They watched the lean, bony man spring under his strange bright metal parasol. The fellow not only seated himself under the shelter, but he produced a cord and tied it from his neck to the shaft.

"He's sure afraid of gettin' out from under that bumbershoot by accident," Monk grunted.

Doc Savage eased back from their point of vantage.

"We have to get out of here!" he said, crisply.

"Huh?" Renny boomed.

"Run for it," Doc advised.

NOT entirely sure what was about to happen, but having a grisly suspicion, they began to run. The siren signal, of course, had been a warning of something to come. Hearing it, the look-out, for such he must be, had taken shelter under the unique parasol.

It came. At first, they thought they were getting hot because they were running. Then they realized the sun had apparently assumed an almost incredible brightness. Not only could they not look directly at the sun, something which had been easy a few moments before, but they could not even gaze at the sky itself.

"That infernal heat!" Ham said, grimly.

They kept running. It was difficult now. They slipped and fell so often that they were wet from the melted snow water which lay everywhere in depressions.

A shot whacked out behind them. Then another. They were distant. No bullets drifted near. The shooting increased.

Doc paused to listen. "Some of their prisoners are trying to escape."

"That makes it different," growled Monk.

"It does."

They did not continue their flight, but waited until they had ascertained, by the drift of the gunfire noises, the route being taken by the flight. Then they moved to intersect the scrap.

They were perspiring freely. The parkas were very uncomfortable and Monk started to remove his.

"Leave it on," Doc advised. "The rays may be stopped to some extent by the clothing."

"Rays!" Monk exploded. "You mean that they've got some kind of a death-ray machine?"

"No," Doc corrected. "The rays which we feel are coming from the sun."

Renny rumbled, "Holy cow! You don't mean to say something screwy is happening to the sun?"

Doc did not answer, for the reason that he caught sight, at that moment, of the cause of the shooting.

JOHNNY, Long Tom, Thurston H. Wardhouse and Velma Crale were fleeing, in a compact group, across the bleak Antarctic wastes.

Horse-faced Derek Flammen and his crowd pursued them. They carried the fantastic-looking parasols. The fugitives had none.

"We'll join Long Tom and the others," Doc said. "We have nothing to lose."

They changed their course. A moment later, the other fugitives saw them and also altered their route. Before long, the two little groups converged.

There was shooting from the men behind, but none of it accurate enough to do more than cause some acute worry. The pursuers were too far back. However, there was no accounting for bad luck, and a slug might hit one of them at any instant.

The heat was terrific.

Long Tom waved his arms, yelled delightedly when he saw them.

Thurston H. Wardhouse stared at Renny, aghast. "I thought you were dead!"

"Not that I know of," Renny boomed.

"I got into a spat with Slagg," Wardhouse explained. "He said you had been killed and the rest of the prisoners would get the same treatment, unless I did what they directed me to do and didn't give them an argument. So we made a break after we decided we would all be killed eventually, anyway."

"Why in thunder should Slagg tell you that?"

"To scare me. But it back-fired on him."

Doc said, "It might be a good idea if we saved our breath and ran."

Velma Crale said, "Yes. We can travel as fast or faster than any of that crowd."

They ran.

Doc asked, "How far will this zone of heat extend, Wardhouse?"

"Ten miles, maybe, darn it!" said Wardhouse.

Monk waved an arm upward. "We won't never make the ten miles. Listen."

They could all hear what he had heard. An airplane!

THERE was more than one of the airplanes. Three of them, if the multiple roar of the motors was any guide. It was impossible to look upward in the strangely heat-irritated sky.

"Don't try it!" Wardhouse warned. "Your eyes may be permanently damaged. Cheaters Slagg damaged his eyes by looking at the sky. That is why he wears those colored spectacles."

Doc said, "It seems that the heat would have become strong enough now to overcome us."

"Yes," said Thurston H. Wardhouse. "I didn't expect us to get this far."

The airplanes were coming closer.

Doc asked, "Penetration of the entire spectrum of cosmic rays is expedited by the use of electromagnetic propulsions from their equipment?"

"From the same apparatus which was aboard the boat," Thurston H. Wardhouse agreed. "They flew it to the valley and I set it up."

Monk was goggling. "Doc! You know what this heat is?"

The bronze man nodded.

"Explain," Monk requested. "I'd almost die happy if the thing was cleared up."

Doc dropped back alongside the homely chemist, said, "It has long been known that the atmosphere layer around the earth stops a great many rays from the sun. Some of these rays are harmless, and others are believed to be capable of producing death or serious injury to the human body."

"I know that," Monk said. "They are known to be very powerful, some of them."

"There is a theory," Doc said, "that these cosmic rays are stopped to some extent by the presence of an electro-magnetic condition in the stratosphere. In other words, a strata of electrification.

"The particles of air, for instance, are made up, according to the Schroedinger theory, of atoms which in turn consist of pulsating spheres of electricity. These either absorb or reflect the light rays. At any rate, it is certain many lengths of light rays do not pass."

Monk blinked. "Then these fellows have——"

"Have an apparatus for changing the characteristics of a limited section of atmosphere above the earth to permit the entrance, through this atmosphere blanket, of the cosmic rays," Doc finished. "This heat we feel is actually a bombardment of cosmic rays."

"I don't see how they could do it," said Monk, who was not exactly without a knowledge of electricity as applied to science. "How'd you figure this all out, Doc?"

"On the dirigible, as we flew south," the bronze man explained.

"But who perfected the contraption?" Monk wanted to know.

Thurston H. Wardhouse answered that. He was breathing heavily; his words came in bunches.

"I did—was experimenting with device—to permit light to pass through fog—boon to aviation."

He was silent for a few moments, catching his breath.

"One day—had contraption turned on," he resumed. "Noticed it got hot. Later on—went to Derek Flammen. Figured he was explorer and scientist—might finance me. He did. Wanted device developed to make heat, though. Didn't know what it was for. Developed it. Went to England to buy parts for apparatus.

"Velma Crale cabled me truth. I demanded cut from

Flammen and Slagg. Still didn't know they planned any killing. Maybe they didn't. But they started out killing. And they held up that liner to get me—and here we are."

The three planes came moaning down in the sky. Their roar was punctuated by loud whackings and gobblings. Small objects began hitting the ground very hard.

"Machine guns!" Ham yelled.

Wardhouse gulped, "I didn't think—they'd kill me."

"And why not?" Monk wanted to know.

"They don't know how—to repair the apparatus—if it goes bad," said Wardhouse.

THE fleeing group did not fling themselves flat, although it might have seemed this would be a good idea. The fact was that they were really smaller targets when running, and any delay would let the mob behind come closer.

With a banshee howl in trio, the planes sank downward. The machine guns gobbled. The ski landing gears all but smashed upon the fugitives.

"We're blamed near helpless!" Renny boomed, wrathfully.

He was right. But they all had noticed that none of the machine gun bullets had hit close. The reason for this was soon apparent.

There was the noise of one of the planes landing ahead and a bit to the left. So brilliant were the cosmic rays, so agonizing upon the delicate tissue of their eyes, they could only squint at the plane after it landed. It did not come close enough to encourage them to rush it.

The craft was a cabin ship, single-motored. The top of the cabin was covered with the shiny metal which seemed to be a shield against the cosmic rays.

The cabin window opened. The voice of horse-faced Derek Flammen reached them.

"I'm offering you a deal!" he hollered loudly from the plane.

"Wait," Doc Savage rapped.

His party came to a stop.

"We need Wardhouse!" shouted Flammen. "Give yourselves up, and we'll keep all of you alive as long as Wardhouse does what he's told to do!"

There was a brief silence.

"They will, too," said Wardhouse, sourly. "I've purposefully kept details of the apparatus from them. They can't do any good without me. And they did do what they said they would before."

"I don't trust 'em!" Monk growled.

"Nobody does," Doc Savage said. "But it narrows down to a question of whether we can make good our escape now. It is obvious that we cannot do so."

Monk groaned. "Then we gotta take 'em up!"

"We have," Doc agreed, quietly.

The bronze man turned in the direction of the plane.

"All right," he called.

"Stick there until the mob comes up!" yelled Flammen elatedly.

The mob came up very shortly. They were mad, cursing, and for a few moments it seemed there would be some shooting. But Flammen put a stop to that.

"We gotta have this guy Wardhouse," he said. "We can operate the contraption, but when something goes wrong, we can't make the repairs. And something is always going wrong."

The prisoners were hauled under the strange mushroomlike umbrellas of metal. The change was startling. The cosmic rays were shut off to a great extent, and it was possible to look about without too much squinting.

"Umbrellas to keep off the sun," one of the mob leered. "Boy, you need 'em, what I mean!"

"And what I mean, you'll need more than an umbrella to keep me off you when my day comes!" Monk promised him.

They walked toward the ridge and over it, and Renny, who was looking forward to seeing the valley, saw it. But he was disappointed.

"Holy cow!" he rumbled. "I don't see nothin' around this place that makes it so valuable!"

Chapter XXI

DEATH OVERHEAD

THE valley was not spectacular. It was not deep, did not have steep sides, and was not dotted with boulders or anything else out of the ordinary. It was just a valley which must have—prior to the apparatus which, by casting a concentration of electromagnetic waves into the sky, caused the admission of strong cosmic rays—been more or less filled with snow.

Not all of the snow had melted. In fact, only a portion of it had, and the water stood in the lower parts of the valley in small lakes.

On the opposite side, on high ground, several huts had been built. They were ordinary structures, except that they had roofs of the shiny metal which was a composition that kept out the cosmic rays.

Seeing the roof shields caused Monk to give close attention to the umbrellas which the captors carried. They were made from the same metal. He decided it was an alloy of lead with a background of some mirrorlike stuff, perhaps chromium, or possibly ordinary mirror silvering with an overcoat of some transparent, flexible substance similar to cellophane.

The party reached the huts, which had been hastily constructed. Near by were partially completed walls of stone and mortar, evidently for permanent shelters.

"Looks as if they expected to stick here some time," Monk offered.

"They do," said Thurston H. Wardhouse. "To strip the valley may require years, if it is done properly. And these fellows are not the kind who will be satisfied until they have everything."

"What are they after?" Monk demanded, eagerly.

CHEATERS SLAGG stepped up with a rifle in his hands. He reversed the rifle, and holding it by the barrel, swung the stock against the side of Monk's head. Monk was knocked out from under the big umbrella beneath which he had been walking, and he fell heavily.

He got up, shaking his head.

"Hell!" grunted Slagg, amazed that the homely chemist had not been knocked out.

"I can take plenty," Monk gritted, and prepared to rush.

"If you get funny, you'll have to take this." Slagg pointed his rifle at Monk.

"Take it easy, Monk," Doc Savage said, and Monk relaxed.

They were halted before the shacks.

Derek Flammen came up and stood scratching his jaw, indecision on his long horselike face.

"Might as well make them useful," he said.

The prisoners were lashed together with a stout rope which ran from one neck to another. They were given parasols, and told to carry rocks suitable for setting in concrete to make the walls of houses. They were struck whenever they attempted to talk, so they did not talk.

They spent ten hours at the task, which was not easy. They were near exhaustion. Their hands were bleeding.

"Sort of tamed down, aren't you?" Cheaters Slagg asked them sarcastically.

Cheaters then eyed Doc Savage. But the bronze man seemed fully as exhausted as the others.

The prisoners were shoved into one of the crude shacks. The men were searched thoroughly. A guard took his position at the entrance.

The shack was open, and the wind, which was now blowing rather strongly, whistled through the apertures. The floor was muddy, for the frost of ages was coming up out of the ground. The prisoners stood about, propped against the walls, dozing, not quite far enough gone to lie down in the mud.

Their haggard faces could be seen from outside.

"THEY'RE beginning to look as if they wish they'd never stuck their beaks into this, don't they?" Cheaters Slagg chuckled from a spot some distance away.

Derek Flammen nodded slowly. He took Slagg's elbow. "I want to talk to you."

"Eh?"

"Private."

They withdrew a number of yards, where their voices would not possibly carry to the hut where the prisoners were quartered. Standing under their umbrella shield, they faced the shack, to be doubly certain the captives did not overhear, and held their consultation.

"Keeping them around is going to be a lot of trouble," said Derek Flammen, a satyr expression on his horse face.

"Uh-huh." Cheaters grinned, realizing something was coming.

"The bronze guy is sure to figure some way of getting clear if we do keep him here," continued Flammen. "He is really a remarkable fellow in his way."

"Uh-huh."

"If we could make Wardhouse think they were alive, we would be ahead to get rid of them."

"Uh-huh."

"Can't you say anything but that?"

"Sure. How we gonna do it?"

"Pretend to send them to the ship by plane, then shoot them when they are out of sight of this valley."

"But how about fooling Wardhouse?"

"We'll tell him to rig up a secret code between Doc Savage's men and himself, so that they can send a radio message to him at intervals to show they are alive. The code word will show whether they are alive or dead."

"Won't it?"

"Sure. Only we will beat the code out of them, and use it to keep Wardhouse pegging away."

"Slick," grinned Slagg.

"Absolutely greasy," chuckled Derek Flammen.

They separated, each walking under his own parasol.

Doc Savage, standing inside the hut, at a point where he had been able to watch the two schemers drew air into his great chest. "They plan to kill us."

"Huh?" Monk gasped. "How d'you know?"

"Slagg and Flammen just talked it over."

"But how——" Monk pointed. "They were way over there?"

"Not too far away to read their lips," Doc reminded.

"I'll be superamalgamated!" murmured bony, big-worded Johnny, who had said almost nothing of late. "This calls for exacerbative cerebration."

"Eh?" said Velma Crale.

"He means that it calls for fast thinking," translated Monk.

The young woman smiled ravishingly at Monk.

"I hope you stick around to translate."

"Cut the comedy!" growled the man with the rifle.

TIME dragged. As far as they could see, no preparations were going forward to fly the prisoners to their death.

"I won't stand for your getting out of my sight, of course!" growled Wardhouse.

"How long you think you can get away with this high-handed stuff?" Monk asked him.

"A long time," the good-looking Wardhouse retorted confidently. "You see, I don't make any adjustments when they are around where they can watch me."

The guard in the door scowled.

"What's in the valley?" Monk asked.

The guard said, "You birds separate and stand with your faces to the wall and the first one who pipes is hereby promised a whack over the bean."

A bit later in the day—it was still the long Antarctic day—Slagg and Flammen appeared with their bland plan to take the prisoners back to the *Uncle Penguin,* where, it was explained, they would be more comfortable.

Doc Savage repeated, almost word for word, the conversation which the two leaders had held. They went off, looking at each other queerly.

After they had gone, the girl spoke for a time, telling how she had met disaster in the dirigible. The craft had been sighted, it seemed, and the planes had flown to the attack.

"I wasn't familiar enough with the controls to do much good," she finished. "I gathered from looking at the dirigible that it was equipped for rocket propulsion or something, but I could have no luck getting the things in operation."

The guard made her become silent.

Slagg and Flammen returned. They issued sharp orders, and the prisoners were separated, each being confined to a shack by himself.

"Sort of discourages any scheming," Flammen explained.

Doc Savage was consigned to the stoutest cubicle, and two guards were always on duty at the door.

AT intervals, Wardhouse was brought to the cubicle and permitted to observe that the prisoners were still alive. Evidently he was doing this at his own insistence.

Time passed. There was considerable activity in the vicinity. Digging. Work with hammers and saws. A dam was constructed in the valley. It was not large. Near by, a large gasoline pressure pump was erected. Quantities of hose were attached.

Doc could see these preparations from his prison. He and the others were not made to work. The captors probably considered this too dangerous.

Came the time when Wardhouse, making one of his rounds under guard to see that the prisoners were alive, spoke to Doc Savage. He did not speak aloud. He merely formed words with his lips, knowing that the bronze man could understand them.

"Hell to pay," Wardhouse said. "They hid themselves in the machine shack and have been watching me adjust the apparatus. I didn't know it. I think they know how to adjust the stuff themselves now."

"Sure?" Doc Savage asked.

"Yes," said Wardhouse with his lips. "They will probably make the adjustments themselves for a day or two to make sure they are onto them. Then they will get rid of us."

The next day, Wardhouse did not come. Nor did he appear the day following.

Doc Savage stood in the rear of his prison shack. He knew very well that Wardhouse had been right. Flammen and Slagg were testing their new knowledge, and it would not be long before they acted.

From where he stood, the bronze man could look through the open door and see the only two members of their party which were permitted their liberty. These were the pig, Habeas Corpus, and Ham's unusual-looking simian, Chemistry.

Habeas and Chemistry were either remarkably intelligent, or perhaps the cosmic rays caused enough physical pain to point out the proper course to them. At any rate, both animals remained almost continuously under shelter.

Standing where he was, Doc Savage began to make strange sounds.

THEY were weird, those sounds, being a combination of cacklings and gurglings, rather difficult to produce. As a whole, they were not unmusical. To all but a minimum of the human population of the world, they would have been absolutely meaningless. A few erudite archaeologists would have recognized the gutturals as words belonging to the Mayan tongue.

Doc was speaking the ancient Mayan which he and his men used for private communication. He was speaking it loudly, and he had no doubt that the other prisoners would be able to hear. They would understand.

After a bit, the emphasis of his words changed. They became cajoling. It sounded as if he were urging a course of action.

Then he fell silent.

The two guards at Doc's shack were both staring inside. They had their guns ready, and were alert.

Doc began to act queerly. He made strange, meaningless gestures with his hands, and started doing a dance that consisted of bending slightly from the hips and straightening, over and over again.

"He's gone nuts," muttered one of the guards.

"Yeah," said the other. "What'd we better do? Shoot him?"

"Call Flammen," advised the first.

They did not call Flammen. Instead, both emitted loud cries and sprang into the air.

It was doubtful if they ever did know exactly what had

happened, for Doc Savage was upon them with flashing speed. He wasted no time. This chance was the last, the most desperate, and he was taking it because no other alternative offered. It was that or wait for death.

Striking with his fists, Doc reached the first of the two guards. No man could stand up under the impact of the corded bronze knuckles; at least no man ever had. The guard fell.

The second guard fired one shot, which climbed straight into the sky. Then he flung his arms about madly, trying to loosen the terrific pressure which had clamped upon his neck. After a bit, he went into a sleeplike paralysis induced by the pressure of Doc's fingers, expertly placed, upon certain spinal nerve centers.

Doc dropped the man.

Habeas Corpus and Chemistry bounded back from underfoot. The two animals had been responsible for the startling of the guards.

Monk and Ham had spent countless hours teaching their respective pets to obey unusual commands given in the tongue of ancient Maya.

Chapter XXII

BEDLAM

DOC SAVAGE was running. He did no shouting, and he kept low, devoting all of his energies to speed. The other prisoners must have overheard his previous speech in Mayan. He had told them what he planned on attempting, and advised them to make breaks during the excitement, if they could.

Doc knew the location of the shack which held Renny. He glanced toward it. The guard was trying to get a bead on Doc with a rifle.

The bronze man carried with him a pistol which had been in the possession of one of the guards. He lifted the weapon. The fact that he never carried a firearm of his own was no indication that he was a tyro in the use of weapons. He had spent more hours practicing marksmanship than the average stenographer spends trying to perfect the use of a typewriter.

The pistol went off and the guard's left leg buckled and he fell down howling. Renny came out and silenced the howling with one swing of an enormous fist.

Guns were whacking. Bullets searched for the bronze man. He weaved from side to side.

The machinery for projecting the magnetic waves into the sky was located over a small ridge. Doc topped the rise, saw the structure and headed for it.

THE building was circular, in the nature of a stockade with a roof which could be shoved into place in case of a storm. The disturbing of the natural balance of temperatures in the region made violent storms almost certain. Hence the precaution, and the stout construction of the machinery house.

A gasoline engine with a large number of cylinders was turning rapidly inside the building. A generator's whine furnished background for the exhaust noise.

Doc reached the door, which was low and square, and dived in.

Two men sprang up, lifting guns. Guards! They must have missed hearing the shooting outside due to the considerable bedlam the gasoline engine and generators were making.

Doc threw his pistol, and it became the pin over which one guard hinged. Air came out of the fellow's mouth and nostrils with a *swish* distinctly audible over the noise of the machinery. The second guard, having difficulty getting the safety of his gun in the firing position, tried to retreat.

He made only one pace backward before a metallic fist found his jaw. The man fell and lost his gun, but was not knocked senseless, since the blow had been a glancing one. He got up and ran. Doc leaped after him, saw something, and veered to the right.

Derek Flammen and Cheaters Slagg were in the rear. Thurston H. Wardhouse was with them. Flammen and Slagg were armed.

They started shooting.

DOC SAVAGE, leaping to the right, gained the cover of the big generator. Not even a tank rifle would reach him through the generator. But it was only temporary shelter.

"Take the right!" Flammen yelled.

"O. K., chief!" shouted Slagg.

Feet pounded in the rear of the enclosure. Doc could not hear them, but he could feel the slight vibration on the floor, through the more even tremor made by the generator.

Then Slagg began to howl curses.

"What is it?" Flammen bawled.

"My glasses!" Slagg squawked. "This damn Wardhouse knocked 'em off, and the light hurts my eyes until I can't see——"

A blow cut short his complaint.

Doc reached for a metal box standing near by, and turned it over. Tools. He took a hammer in his right hand, a Stillson wrench, heavy pliers and a cold chisel in his left. They were the weightiest tools in the box.

He threw the hammer at Flammen the instant he saw him. Flammen was agile, and on guard. He ducked. Simultaneously, he shot, but the slug went wide. He tried to shoot again, and Doc threw the Stillson, which Flammen dodged. He did not dodge the pliers, however. They hit his shoulder and caused him to drop his gun.

Flammen ran backward.

Wardhouse and Slagg were going over and over on the floor like a cat and dog. Flammen stopped to kick Wardhouse in the head. Wardhouse fell limp. Flammen picked Slagg up and ran with him out of a rear door.

The moment Flammen and Slagg were out of the door, bullets began coming in.

Doc Savage angled to one side, reached the door without being harmed, and banged it shut. Then he looked around.

The enclosure walls had been constructed for security, both against the elements and against bullets. It was probable that Flammen and Slagg had feared that Doc and his aides might get a chance to fire into the place, so the walls had been made leadproof. That would come in handy now.

Doc went to Wardhouse. The man had a bullet hole through his thigh. He must have been hit while senseless by one of the slugs which had come through the door. Blood was not coming in dangerous quantities.

Doc straightened and whipped a glance over the place. It was the first time he had seen the apparatus.

It was about what he had expected. The waves, of course, were created by apparatus which did not differ greatly in appearance from the mechanism of an extremely powerful radio transmitter. There was even an aërial, but a rather differently shaped one, sprawled above the center. It resembled a circular cobweb of copper bars.

There were vacuum tubes, innumerable coils and condensers, and black panels holding meters with quivering needles.

Doc gathered up the weapons which the defeated quartet had dropped, and went to the door.

His aides were fighting their way toward the wave projection plant.

ALL of them had succeeded in breaking from the shacks where they were held. No doubt Renny had been a great help there. The big-fisted engineer was an excellent shot.

Doc Savage, shooting slowly and accurately, emptied one after another of his guns. His shooting was remarkable. He inflicted no wounds which, with ordinary care, were dangerous. The guns were unfamiliar, and each was different. He missed only twice. That was because the sight alignment of two of the guns was off.

The firing was effective, and his aides piled through the door.

"Blazes!" Monk puffed. "We're here, but what good's it gonna do us?"

He did not wait for an answer, but picked up his pig, Habeas, by an ear and shook him, by way of showing affection.

Thurston H. Wardhouse tried to get to his feet, having regained his senses. He groaned loudly, grabbed his wound and sank back to the damp floor.

Doc Savage went to Wardhouse. "The projector is not running full strength, is it?"

Wardhouse squinted at the meters. "No."

"If it is turned on full force, will it make a great deal of difference?" Doc asked. "Will it cause more cosmic rays to penetrate the atmosphere?"

"A lot more."

Renny boomed, "Holy cow! C'mere, Doc!"

Renny was stealing glances through the door and Doc joined him.

"Look," Renny said.

They could, from where they stood, see down the valley to what seemed to be an excavation of considerable extent. Hose lines ran to this, and long, narrow troughs had been constructed.

"I get this," Renny boomed. "It was the only way they could get the stuff. Flying it to the coast would be too expensive before it was extracted. They had to have water to work the beds, and it stays froze up here the year around, so there was probably no water until they worked out this contraption to get some heat."

Monk came over and looked. "A placer mine! They're working a gravel bed with a hydraulic stream and sluice boxes."

Renny called, "Wardhouse?"

"Yes?"

"What are these birds placering?"

"Platinum," Wardhouse said. "There's a little gold, too. Didn't you know?"

"No," said Renny. "But I seem to remember that I've been trying to find out."

Wardhouse started to make some reply, but listened instead. Derek Flammen was yelling.

"We've got bombs in the planes!" Flammen was howling. "Come out of there, or we'll blow you all to hell!"

THE threat was blunt and left nothing to argue about.

Monk muttered, "Maybe we can wing their planes——"

"Don't be silly," Ham snapped. "Not with rifles. Not three planes."

Flammen bawled from outside somewhere, "I ain't

gonna hooligan around waiting for an answer! Is it yes or no?"

Doc Savage went swiftly to Wardhouse. "I'll lift you up. Help me increase the radiation of the apparatus."

Wardhouse gritted his teeth as Doc supported him, and began to manipulate knobs. The wail of the generator took on a labored note, and the engine throttle was opened to the last notch. Meter indicators crawled over toward the red sectors which meant an overload. Doc Savage did quite a bit of the manipulating of controls himself.

"Good night!" Wardhouse grunted. "You seem to know a heck of a lot about how this device works!"

Doc said, "Experimented along this line myself. How long have you been working with this system?"

"Few months. Why?"

"Unless I am mistaken greatly," Doc told him, "there are burns being inflicted on every one exposed. These burns are not apparent, at first, but crop up later, in the manner of some types of radium poisoning, and require treatment."

"Been afraid of that," admitted Wardhouse. "I wanted to experiment a lot more with the system, but Flammen and Slagg kept pushing me."

Outside, Flammen howled, "What d'you say in there? We don't want to ruin our contraption to get rid of you, but we sure as hell will if we have to!"

Doc Savage took up a position near the door. He was very careful to keep under the arrangement of overhead shields which sheltered a part of the enclosure which held the apparatus.

Their enemies seemed to be growing very uncomfortable under their shielding parasols. They were squirming about. Many had arms across their eyes.

An increased bombardment of cosmic rays was arriving. And there would be more later.

Doc made his powerful voice loud enough to carry to all of the besiegers.

"You have possibly half an hour to live," he said. "The machine, which has been working at only part strength, is now on full power."

Flammen howled, "You can't do that!"

Something about that statement struck Monk as funny. He hooted a laugh.

"I'd like to know why not?" he yelled at Flammen.

Doc Savage withdrew and grasped the topmost sheet from a pile of shield metal which was stacked at one end of the enclosure.

"Lend a hand," he directed. "We'll have to rig thicker shields for ourselves."

The others fell to. They were beginning to feel the need of the shields. Their heads were aching, their eyes almost refusing to function, and their skin was hot.

Outside, Derek Flammen began to bawl frenzied orders.

"Get the planes into the air!" he squawled. "Bomb the place before the cosmic rays get us down!"

INSIDE the machine stockade—for it was actually a stockade with a roof over portions—the besieged did not pause in the task of rigging thicker shields beneath which they could crouch.

But Renny rumbled, "I don't savvy this business of the cosmic rays increasing gradually. They're light, ain't they? And don't light travel at a hundred and eighty-six thousand miles a minute or something?"

Wardhouse gritted his teeth against the pain of his wound. "The gradual increase is a deceptive sensation. The full bombardment of cosmic rays comes almost instantly after the apparatus is turned on.

"But it takes a little time for the air to warm. And the cosmic rays do not, when arriving full strength, strike down a person instantly. On the contrary, the effect is cumulative, taking time, like a sunburn. A little exposure is not necessarily lethal."

The sound of a plane's motor reached their ears. It warmed only briefly, then a change in the quality of the sound indicated the ship had taken off.

"Rifle!" Doc Savage said, crisply.

A rifle—the only one they had—was handed him. He took up a position atop the generator, a vantage point from which he could see the plane approaching.

"But you can't look against these cosmic rays to aim!" Monk wailed. "The things are too blinding!"

Doc called to Wardhouse, "Cut off the radiation the moment you see my arm wave."

Wardhouse nodded and took up a position at the controls.

Doc waited. He could not see the plane; it was impossible to see anything but an eye-hurting glare when looking upward. He had to judge by the sound of the motor how close the aircraft was, and finally he waved his arm.

Wardhouse shut off the radiation. Instantly, it was possible to see, proving that the cosmic rays did cease penetrating the instant the device was not in operation.

Doc aimed quickly, fired. Nothing happened to the plane. It was unpleasantly close. He fired again. Again. A fourth time.

The plane's motor stopped.

WHAT happened next would not have occurred had the pilot of the plane not thought too suddenly about saving his own skin. He banked wildly, thinking perhaps that his motor had conked of its own accord, and intending to get back to the landing field while he still had gliding speed.

And Wardhouse turned the radiation on again.

Doc Savage, who was watching the plane, involuntarily gasped and clutched his eyes when the terrific blaze of cosmic emanation struck his pupils. He leaped hurriedly from the generator and got under the thick shield which they had rigged.

Effect of the burst of blinding rays on the pilot of the plane was the fellow's undoing. Blinded, he could not see what he was doing. He failed to level off enough after his turn, and went into a slip. He mistook the slip for a dive, yanked up, overcontrolled, and went into a spin.

He hit in the valley. Hit and went up again—in a cloud of smoke and flame. The explosive with which the plane was laden went off under the shock. The earth shook for miles and the plane fragments came drifting down, after a time, over an expanse of acres.

Chapter XXIII

TRICK COIN

THEY got a hail after a while.

Some men wanted to surrender. They were a terrified crowd. They were afraid to try to take off in the planes—the two that remained—because nobody could see. The light was too blinding. The eyes did not seem to become accustomed to it. They knew they could not flee the vicinity before they were overcome.

"Send Derek Flammen and Cheaters Slagg in alone first!" Doc ordered.

"Can't," came the reply.

"Why not?"

"They were in the plane that blew up."

Doc Savage glanced at the spot where the plane had gone to pieces. It was a question whether they would ever find identifiable portions of Cheaters Slagg and Derek Flammen.

He let the men surrender.

Later, he flew in a plane to the ice barrier, caught the *Uncle Penguin,* and terrorized the three men aboard, threatening to drop bombs on them. They surrendered meekly enough.

The business of transferring Flammen's mob to the ship, where they would be imprisoned and taken north to become patients in Doc Savage's remarkable criminal curing institution in up-State New York, took time. Renny flew one plane. Monk and Ham alternated flying the other.

Doc Savage made an examination and assay of the platinum and gold deposits. Slagg and Flammen had indicated, long ago, that they would run into millions, and they were not far wrong.

Doc suggested a division—a share to the girl, Velma Crale, a share to Thurston H. Wardhouse, whose inventive genius had been so misused, and the remainder and lion's share to be converted eventually to the credit of a certain international charity foundation which was noted for its good work.

VELMA CRALE turned down her share. "I wouldn't feel right," she explained.

The young woman, now that she had lost her desire for a share of the Antarctic wealth, had become a very nice person. Ravishing, in fact. Clever, witty. It was to be suspected that she was turning on her charm for the benefit of Doc Savage, but Doc was immune, as far as outward appearances went.

There must be, he had determined long ago, no feminine entanglements in his existence. They were too dangerous. Enemies would strike at him through any one he chanced to love.

Doc devoted his time to working with the radiation apparatus invented by Wardhouse. Wardhouse was, Doc discovered, one of the most promising of modern scientists, and after Wardhouse turned down a share of the platinum, the bronze man determined to finance the fellow in future experiments.

They learned one thing about the radiation device—it was dangerous in a sneaking, unexpected way. Or rather, the cosmic rays were. But it was not until weeks later that they realized this, when they began to suffer from burns which were painful, but fortunately, not incurable.

To make use of the heat, the radiation mechanism would have to be operated from remotely situated points, with no workmen in the zone of heat. This limited use of the thing to the summer season, when the water needed for placer mining the platinum would not freeze too quickly after the apparatus was shut off to permit workmen to return.

But months were required for this angle to develop, and when they were preparing to leave the platinum valley on the Antarctic continent, Monk and Ham had another of their interminable spats. This one was different in that it had a somewhat abrupt ending.

The argument started over who should fly attractive Velma Crale back to the *Uncle Penguin*. It raged heatedly. Finally, Monk had an idea.

"Match you," he offered, producing his coin which had tails on both sides.

"O. K.," Ham agreed.

Monk flipped the coin.

"Heads," Ham said.

"I win," Monk chuckled, and walked off, putting the coin in his pocket.

His pocket had a hole, and the coin went through. Ham picked it up, looked closely at the bit of deceptive money. Ham then picked up a monkey wrench, wrapped his scarf around the heavy end, calmly walked around in front of Monk, and knocked the homely chemist senseless.

"Heads," the dapper lawyer said to the dreaming Monk, "is what you'll have when you wake up."

To the world at large, Doc Savage is a strange, mysterious figure of glistening bronze skin and golden eyes. To his fans he is the greatest adventure hero of all time, whose fantastic exploits are unequaled for hair-raising thrills, breathtaking escapes, blood-curdling excitement!

- ☐ S7637 **THE DERRICK DEVIL** (75¢)
- ☐ S7492 **THE SEVEN AGATE DEVILS** (75¢)
- ☐ S7229 **THE METAL MASTER** (75¢)
- ☐ S6912 **THE MAD MESA** (75¢)
- ☐ S6653 **THE MOTION MENACE** (75¢)
- ☐ S6725 **THE GREEN DEATH** (75¢)
- ☐ S6923 **THE FRECKLED SHARK** (75¢)
- ☐ S5947 **THE LIVING FIRE MENACE** (75¢)
- ☐ S6542 **THE SUBMARINE MYSTERY** (75¢)
- ☐ S5838 **THE YELLOW CLOUD** (75¢)